Eternal Shadows
Willow Asteria

For those of you who feel
swallowed by the dark...

Know that light will always shine
through.

Content Warning

P lease be advised that this book may not be suitable for all audiences.

This book contains sexual content, death, blood, graphic violence, oppressive government, non-consensual imprisonment and forced captivity, torture, mentions of physical and verbal abuse, brief child abuse, and other topics some readers may not find suitable.

One

For the first time in a hundred years, the people of Gaylwynn saw the sun, and their hearts quaked with fear. This omen meant only one horrifying thing. War was coming once again.

Squinting my eyes, I could not help but stare up at the sun. Everyone in the market stopped and stared up at the sky. The darkness that surrounded the sun faded away, and the black clouds cleared, revealing a bright blue sky. What was normally a bustling street fell silent. This could only mean one thing.

King Marcellus Vespero was dead.

He was only one hundred and thirty, which was so young for a wielder of elemental power. Those with magic in their blood lived for centuries. But I would not shed a single tear for his early demise.

Looking around the market, I saw so many people barely getting by. Farmers who had pathetic yields of shriveled fruits, vegetables, and barely any meat to sell. Families that were skin and bone because there wasn't enough food to go around. The King made sure that our land stayed barren so that we relied on the goods of the capital city of Vaylnn.

Goods that were too expensive for most people to afford.

Many who lived in my village worked in the capital, as it was so close. Even though my guardian and I both worked at the royal library in the city, we could never afford the luxuries that so many citizens of the capital could. It was hard enough getting what we needed, let alone things we wanted.

Something under my skin tingled as I felt the warmth of the sun for the first time in my entire life. A burst of energy filled me, and a smile grew on my face.

While I still had many errands to run, who knew how much longer we had before the sun vanished, and I needed to soak in as much as I could. I craved it, needed it, more than air. For the first time, I felt *alive*.

Rushing home, I raced to the meadow behind our cottage and laid in the plush grass. A sigh escaped my lips, and for the first time ever, I felt at peace.

Unfortunately, that peace would not last long.

When the monarch died, the elements had to battle to determine who would rule next. They sent one representative from each element through deadly challenges until only one was left standing.

With its only weakness snuffed out, darkness has ruled over the land for the last three Coronation cycles. With no light bringers left since the last one died in the previous Coronation ritual, we stand no chance of stopping them from winning once again.

For the Prince of Darkness, Sterling Vespero, had trained his entire life under his father, Marcellus, to take the throne once his time came.

It would not be too much longer until the magic that ran through this land chose the other contestants.

Though it would not matter, for none of them would survive the trials. The Prince of Darkness was now the most powerful in the kingdom, and he would do anything to claim the crown and return Gaylwynn to darkness.

When the first dark lurker took the throne, the king used his powers to overshadow the sun. Without the sun, the light bringers stayed weak, as it was the sun's rays that filled their magical well.

Even after the last light bringer fell, the sun never returned.

"Aurora?!" Lucinda, my guardian, called out to me. The panic in her voice made me jolt up.

"Luci? Is everything alright?" My head was on a swivel, searching for her, but she was not in my line of sight.

She rushed from around the front of the house. Once her gaze was locked on mine, she ran toward me. Fear was seeded in her golden eyes. "We have to go! Get up, child."

"What? What's wrong?" Never in my twenty years have I ever seen her so nervous.

Without responding, she grabbed me by the arm and pulled me to my feet. "Hurry, this way!" She guided me to the tree line and into the heavy woods beyond the meadow.

"Lucinda! You're scaring me! What is going on?" I asked again, but my questions were left unanswered.

Tears welled in my eyes as I continued to run with her. She had raised me since I was a baby and was the one person in this world that I trusted. I never knew my real parents; she was the only mother I ever had. Whatever was bothering her had to be something significant.

We lived a quiet life outside the capital city of Vaylnn. Lucinda worked within the city as an archivist for the royal library, and this past year, I began work there as an assistant. We lived peaceful lives. We didn't have any enemies. I could not think of any reason why she would have us running through the woods.

After what seemed like forever, she finally slowed her pace. Her eyes slowly scanned the forest floor. My heart pounded in my chest as the only sound was the crunch of leaves beneath our feet.

"Where is it?" She said as she continued to search the ground. Leaves flew into the air as she pushed them away revealing the bare earth beneath. Frantically, she moved to another spot... and another... and another.

"Can you tell me what is going on?" I yanked away from her.

She stood straight and quickly turned toward me. The fear in her eyes caused my stomach to turn. "Aurora, there is something I need to tell you. Please don't hate me. I had to keep this secret from you. It was your mother's dying wish." Her voice quivered as she spoke.

"You knew my mother? Why did you never tell me this?" I said as anger welled in my core. I did not know Lucinda to keep secrets, and knowing she kept one so big nearly broke my heart.

"I know a lot of things that I haven't told you. Most importantly, you and I are not magicless. We are light bringers, and if I can't find our secret hideaway before the guards find you, it will be too late to stop you from joining the Coronation."

Two

My entire body tensed, and all I could do was stare at her with wide eyes. This had to be a dream — no, a nightmare. There is no way that I was a light bringer. Stepping away from Lucinda, a deep cackle escaped my throat. This had to be some absurd prank she was pulling. "Good one, Lucinda. You really had me going." I looked around, waiting to see if some of our friends from town would jump out and laugh as well. But it was only my voice that echoed off the trees.

She jolted toward me and pressed her hand firmly to my mouth. "Aurora! Will you be quiet? This is not a joke! This is not a game!" Her stare intensified, and as I looked her in the eyes, I saw the signs of age starting to grace her features. I knew when those two wrinkles between her brows showed themselves, she meant business.

I gave her a simple nod in response, and after a short moment, she removed her hand and stepped away, letting out a tense breath. It was unnerving how worked up she was.

"You're serious," I whispered to her. My heart pounded so hard, I swore it was about to leap from my chest.

"More serious than I have been in my entire life." Her tone was so cold with fear it sent a shiver down my spine.

Turning away from me, she continued to scan the ground, using her foot to kick away the leaves and debris. All I could do was watch. My body refused to allow me to move or speak.

After about five minutes of looking, she let out an exasperated sigh. "When the dark started to eliminate the light, we placed safe havens across the land. Hidden bunkers for us to hide when needed," she said as she looked back at me with tears in her eyes.

"Are you sure there is one here? Maybe we are in the wrong spot!" Panic swelled in me. This had to be a dream. No way was this possible. There was no way that I had magic and was about to be dragged into the deadliest competition in the kingdom. I could not believe that this was happening. Watching my guardian search frantically only made me feel worse. She was always so calm and collected. I did not recognize the frantic woman in front of me.

"This is where I hid with you after you were born. I know it is here, but after twenty years, the earth has done an amazing job hiding it."

Shouting in the distance had both of our heads snapping in the direction of the sound. My heart pounded in my chest. I could not understand the words they were saying, but I did make out at least four distinct voices.

"Fuck," Lucinda snarled, "Aurora. Run. Do not look back. No matter what you hear, no matter what, do *not* look back," she snapped at me, then took a step in the direction of the voices.

"You are coming with me!" I demanded. There was no way I could leave her behind. She was my family, and I couldn't imagine life without her.

"There is no time. I will distract them. I cannot allow you to be entered into the Coronation. They will do anything to make sure you are eliminated." She spun toward me and embraced me tightly. "Live, Aurora. Escape and live. I love you. Go!"

I hugged her back with tears welling in my eyes. Too soon, she pulled away from me and ran in the direction of the voices. Silently, I watched her until she vanished into the trees. My heart broke into a million pieces as I heard the shouting get louder.

Wiping the tears from my eyes, I inhaled deeply, spun around, and dashed deeper into the woods. There was no way I would let her sacrifice go to waste. I could not allow myself to think about what was going to happen to Lucinda once she was captured. Only those under thirty-five were able to join the Coronation battle, and at over forty, she was too old. I could not accept that she would meet the same fate as all other light bringers. Since she was not eligible to fight for the crown, I hoped they would allow her to live.

Once the Coronation was over, I would return here. I would save Lucinda. Hopefully, I wouldn't be too late.

I ran as fast as my short legs could carry me. I was never much of a distance runner, and jumping over fallen trees and ducking under thick vines was beginning to take a toll. This run proved one thing: if I were sent to join the Coronation, I would not make it. There were several who trained their entire lives for this and would surely get to me before I could get them. Most of them worked in the King's guard, as he found them to be the most useful there. Never had I met anyone with magic that did not work for the King.

The sound of my heart pounded in my ears as my mind raced. Where was I to go? Never had I left the small village that I called my home. Was there somewhere that I could escape until everything was said and done?

A scream escaped my throat as the ground below my feet split open and I fell into a deep pit. A pain shot up my spine as I landed flat on my ass. Struggling, I stood and wiped the dirt from my pants. When I went over to the dirt walls of the pit, they were perfectly smooth; there was no way I was going to be able to climb out.

"Did you really think you could run, light bringer?" A condescending female voice asked from above.

"Let me free! I am no light bringer!" I called out in response. The ground shook beneath me and formed a cage of thick thorny vines around me. My knees buckled as I steadied myself. The earth's floor rose, forcing me up and out of the pit. The woman finally came into view. Her dark green hair was in a high ponytail, and I knew exactly who she was when our eyes locked and I saw the vertical scar over her left eye.

King Marcellus' captain of the guard, Charoite. One of the most powerful earth shatterers. She and Marcellus battled in the same games that made him king, but he allowed her to live as long as she swore fealty to him. Somehow she looked as if she was in her forties, but she was almost one hundred and twenty years old. For the first time, I wondered what caused Marcellus to die at only one hundred and thirty.

Stepping toward my earthly prison, she looked down at me with a cold expression. It took everything I had not to break down in front of her. I would not show weakness.

"We will see about that. Your guardian is on the way to the capital now to be tested. You will join her. If you are not a light bringer, you will be released."

"And if I am?" I asked softly, my voice shaking.

Charoite knelt and offered me a smirk. Grabbing me by my chin, she forced me to look her in the eyes. "Well, since you claim not to be, no need to worry about that."

Three

The scent of lemongrass and smoke filled the air. Lucinda and I were both kneeling, facing an altar, our hands tied behind our backs. Upon the altar was a bowl of fire with smoke gently rising from it. It was the only source of light in the small square room, and it cast everything in an orange glow. Two guards stood behind us, with their swords drawn. One was an earth shatterer, and the other was a dark lurker. While I was grateful to see Lucinda alive and unharmed, we had not said a single word to each other since we were reunited in this cold, dark room.

A man in a hooded robe came from behind us and walked to the altar.

"This is a quick process," he said without looking at us. Picking up one of the jars, he emptied its contents into the flame, causing it to roar. "They claim you both to be light bringers. For if that is true, it would be a miracle." He said so softly that I barely heard him. Then he turned toward us and lowered his hood. His bright red hair revealed him to be a fire wielder.

Fire used to be an element of passion and strength. Ever since darkness sat upon the throne, they subserviently bent a knee. Now, many of them work within the capital completing rituals, such as this one. I even heard rumors that they had also set fire to many farms in the countryside to make those communities more reliant on the capital's goods. With the destruction of the kingdom on the line, everyone was too scared to try to rebel. I prayed to the heavens no one was that evil.

"Lucinda Wylker, please rise. Face the flame to reveal your truth." His tone was cold and sharp.

Lucinda stood, holding her head high. She did not hesitate as she approached the altar. The fire wielder plucked a single hair from her head and dropped it into the flames. A bright flash of white light filled the room, making the fire wielder squint his eyes and turn away. To my surprise, the bright flash of light caused me no discomfort. I could see everything clearly, and warmth enveloped me.

"Light bringer," one of the guards behind us hissed in disgust.

"Lucinda Wylker, you are a light bringer. While you are too old to join the Coronation, you are under arrest for hiding your element from the crown," said the other guard as he walked in front of me over to her.

"No!" I called out. Panic rose in my chest as I watched helplessly as he removed his blade from it's sheath.

"Wait," said the man in the hooded robes. "If the young one is also a light bringer, she will need a guardian to guide her through the Coronation. It is the law of the land, is it not? We would not want to put the young girl at a disadvantage."

The guard quickly shot a glare in my direction and released Lucinda's arm. "Well, go on with it. Test her!"

"Aurora, please. Step forward. Allow the flames to reveal your truth," the fire wielder instructed calmly.

Slowly, I stood. My gaze was focused on the flame on the altar. The fire danced around the bowl, and embers floated into the air. Taking a deep breath, a deep calm washed over me, and something within me illuminated. For the first time, I accepted what Lucinda told me.

I accepted what the fire would reveal.

I accepted that I was the light that would bring an end to the darkness as warmth filled my soul.

A single strand was plucked from my head, and I refused to flinch. I watched as the ash-blonde strand was dropped into the fire. Bright white light filled the room. Stronger than Lucinda's. It did not dim right away. No, it bathed the room in a glorious glow for a few moments.

Looking toward Lucinda, I saw the smile of someone who knew change was coming.

"Why is the light not dying down?" Asked one of the guards in an aggressive tone.

"I—I," the fire wielder stuttered, "I'm not sure. Never has the reveal lasted this long!"

"You fools," Lucinda finally spoke in a quiet but intense tone. "It is because you are in the presence of the next Queen of Gaylwynn."

Four

As soon as we were declared light bringers, the guards applied shackles to our wrists and ankles, and the iron around my wrist weighed heavy. Iron was used to silence magical abilities, not that it would change anything for me. Never once had I used my magic.

Which was so odd, because at the age of thirteen is when elemental abilities begin to manifest. With proper training, most elementals are proficient in using their magic by the age of eighteen. How could I go seven years without a hint of light energy coming through?

Lucinda and I were dragged to the palace and escorted directly to the throne room. My heart pounded in my chest as we walked through the dark and frigid halls. I tried to reach for Lucinda's hand, but the guard commanded us not to interact with one another. She was one of the only things that brought me hope, not being able to reach out to her for comfort withered my soul. The eyes of portraits of past Kings and Queens seemed to follow me as we progressed. No one spoke a single word as we made our way further inside.

The palace had a haunting beauty to it, even though I hated to admit it. Every piece of artwork was a masterpiece. Every stone archway was perfectly crafted. There was one thing that was missing that made this place seem more like a prison than a castle.

Windows.

There was not a single drop of natural light to be found. Golden sconces lined the walls and cast the palace in a fiery glow.

As we got closer to the throne room, the more opulent the decor became. The sconces turned to crystal chandeliers, and marble statues lined the walls, depicting all the Coronated kings and queens of the past.

Every single light bringer's head was broken off.

Now that King Marcellus was dead, his queen would rule as regent until after the Coronation. She was just as vicious as her late husband and son. There was a reason the King of Darkness chose her to be his bride. Rumor was that she led unsuspecting suitors to her bed, only for them to wind up dead. The King was the only one known to survive her. But that never stopped more from trying to slide into her sheets. Evil and cruelty pair so well together. A shiver trailed down my spine as I thought of the combination of the two of them. Sterling, The Prince of Darkness, would truly be my strongest competition within the Coronation. Honestly, I was not sure how I would win without magic, since I was still unsure how to use it.

But I had no other choice. It was win or die.

I would not be like the others who bent their knees to oppression just to save themselves. I would fight until my dying breath for just a chance to free Gaylwynn from the darkness.

The guard in front of us abruptly stopped and turned toward us. "Wait here," he barked. "I will see if the Queen is ready to see you."

Before anyone could respond, he spun and rushed into the throne room. A sheer red curtain with black embroidery that hung in the doorway waved in the wind of his path.

The second guard came to the front of us and leaned against the dark stone wall, staring at us intensely.

"You two are lucky," he said. "If you weren't needed for the Coronation, you would have met your end instead of meeting the Queen."

Lucinda scoffed in response. "You would never have found us if it weren't for the Coronation."

I tilted my head in confusion. "How were we found?"

The guard chuckled. "You really did keep her dumb. She has no idea about anything, does she? In the private study of the king, there are six crystal spheres. One for each element. Upon the death of the current monarch, it reveals the faces of those who will compete for the crown. Since no one expected the king to die so soon, I guess she didn't think it important to keep you well hidden. As soon as your face was revealed, you were recognized as the librarian's child."

My eyes went wide. This whole time she knew there was a chance of us getting caught. The pain of betrayal rang through my chest.

"I am sorry," Lucinda said in a whisper. "I had to make a choice. Struggle to survive, as so many do out in the country lands, or live close to the capital to keep you comfortable."

The first guard came back through the curtain. "Queen Serena will see you now."

The second guard kicked off the wall and returned to his position behind us. We were taken past the red curtain and into the throne room. Across the massive room, on a dais, was a single golden throne. A wall of red and black sheer curtains was just beyond the throne. Sitting on the black velvet cushion was the most beautiful woman I had ever seen.

Her sleek, long black hair draped down her front. Her tight red gown that showed off her curves had a deep V-cut, accentuating her cleavage. Casually lounging on her throne, she looked as if she had no cares in the world.

The front guard took a step forward, got down on one knee, and bowed his head. "My Queen, these are the light bringers."

Slowly, she stood and stepped down from the dais. "Gaylwynn is no place for light." Her voice dripped with dark and seductive energy, and it made my skin crawl. "Enjoy the sun while you can. Once my son is upon the throne, darkness will reign."

The sound of her heels against the stone echoed in the room. No one else dared make a sound. My breath caught in my throat as she stopped directly in front of me. I refused to look her in the eye. Roughly, she grabbed me by my chin and forced my gaze to match hers. Her ruby-red lips curled into a smirk. My heart pounded in my chest as we stared at each other. She wanted me to cower, I could tell in the vicious gleam in her eyes, but I would not give her the satisfaction.

Aggressively, she released me, spun away, and walked back to her throne. "In three days the others will arrive with their guardians." A light chuckle escaped her throat. "You thought all these years you could hide in the darkness my husband provided. I will teach you what true darkness is like."

Gracefully, she sat back down and leaned back in her seat, her smirk grew wider. Looking over to Lucinda, my heart broke. For it was true fear that I saw in her eyes, even though she tried to hide it.

"Send them to the pit. They can come out when the Coronation has begun." The queen's voice was cold as ice as she spoke.

Rough hands grabbed me and pulled me back, causing me to stumble. Before I fell, they grabbed me tight.

"Come on, light bringer. Let's see how well you do in total darkness," the guard growled.

Five

The iron door to the pit creaked open, and the room filled with an orange glow, revealing the horror I had endured for the past two days. A large circular room with a dirt floor, with prisoners chained to the wall. Lucinda and I were across the room from each other so that we were as far apart as we could be. The iron collar weighed heavy on me.

Several iron rods hung down from a wheel that was on the ceiling. As the guards entered the pit, they circled the room, randomly grabbed prisoners, and threw them toward the center.

"Up, up, up!" They exclaimed as the selected prisoners stood.

One of them stopped in front of me and smirked. "Your turn, light bringer. To the wheel!" He grabbed me by the hair and forced me over to one of the rods. It was far enough that the iron around my neck tightened.

Grabbing hold of the iron bar, I pushed on it, and the wheel slowly started to spin. One of the other prisoners slipped in the dirt and smacked into the rod they were holding onto.

The guards laughed at him. As we pushed the rods, the iron grew tighter around my neck, causing me to nearly choke.

As the wheel spun, the ceiling opened and flooded the room with light from the sun. Hisses and groans filled the room. The bright light seared my vision and caused me to squint. This was the first time the ceiling had been opened since I had arrived at the pit.

"Hope you're all hungry," one of the guards laughed as another guard rolled in a barrel full of scraps.

He dumped it into the dirt. So many of the prisoners rushed toward the pile and fought for the little there was. My stomach turned, and I looked away. I could not believe the conditions we were kept in. Truly, it was barbaric.

No one deserved to be treated this way. There was no rhyme or reason people were sent here, other than displeasing the crown. None of the people I had spoken to were criminals. They were people who missed their families. The old woman who was next to me had been in the pit for the last five years. Her crime? Stealing bread that was going to be thrown away to bring home to her family.

She used to work in the palace kitchens, and what she had taken the king and queen deemed trash.

After a few moments, the guards pushed the prisoners away from the scraps. "That's enough!" Their voices boomed off the stone-cold walls. Whatever was left, they scooped back up into the barrel.

The pleas of the prisoners broke my heart. A young boy approached the guard, begging for more to eat. The guard scoffed at him and pushed him into the dirt.

"Enough! He's just a kid!" I shouted to him.

The room fell silent as all eyes fell on me. The guard scowled and prowled over to me. Grabbing my leash, he pulled it tight, causing the iron collar to dig into my skin.

"He is trash. Like you. In a few days, you will be dead, and our prince will become king. Do not think anything you say matters." Before I could respond, he threw me, and my head smacked against the stone. "Anyone else have something to say?" He looked around the room, awaiting a challenge. When no one answered, he walked over to the iron door. "That's what I thought. Close the wheel!" He demanded.

My vision wobbled as my head throbbed. As I touched my head, I hissed in pain, and when I pulled my hand away to inspect it, red dripped from my fingertips and nausea washed over me.

The prisoners at the wheel closed the ceiling, and once the guards shut the iron door, we were left in total darkness.

I had no idea how much time had passed since the last time guards had visited the pit. The pain had me in and out of consciousness. The mother of the young boy had come over to me to check on my head. She had used her scarf to wrap it up, keeping it away from the dirt and to stop the bleeding.

The door creaked open once again, but this time only a single guard walked in. He immediately shut the door, blocking the tiny bit of light that was able to come in from the hall. It was so dark that I couldn't make out all his features, but I was sure I did not recognize him. His gaze fell to me, and he rushed over to me, staring at me for a moment, in total silence. Every prisoner had their eyes locked on us, and whispers filled the room.

"Get up," he demanded.

Panic welled in my chest, and all I could do was stare up at him. I did not want to incur the wrath of another guard.

"I said get up!" Firmly, but not roughly, he grabbed me by my arm and forced me to my feet. A soft whimper escaped my lips as pain wrung through me. The guard narrowed his eyes at me and loosened his grip, but did not release me. "I am going to unchain you, and you are going to come with me. If you try to run, I will kill you. Understand?"

I nodded in response. I couldn't understand why this guard was doing this. I prayed that he would not harm me further.

"Where are you taking her?!" Lucinda shouted from across the pit.

The guard snapped his head in her direction. "That is none of your concern. The two of you will be reunited before the Coronation begins."

He unlocked the collar around my neck and pulled me into him. A deep sigh of relief escaped my throat as I no longer felt my energy being drained from the iron. The scent of vanilla and bourbon filled my nose. I hated that his touch sent warmth through me. He pushed me forward and guided me out of the pit.

I did not dare to look at Lucinda. If I had, I would have lost all control I had over my emotions, and I would have broken down. I would not allow this man to see me falter.

The sound of the iron door slamming shut behind us caused me to flinch. The guard's grip tightened, and he pulled me down the hallway.

He let out a soft chuckle. "The little star spooks easily, I see."

The nickname he gave me caught me off guard, and I quickly turned my head to him. I was even more confused now, for the first time I was shown kindness in this cruel place. I was not sure if I could trust it. Finally, I could see his face now that we were in the lighted hallway. I hated that he was the most handsome man I had ever seen. His dark hair was in a topknot, short dark hair covered his sharp jaw, and I could drown in his ocean-blue eyes.

A smirk grew on his lips. "Little star, you should work on your poker face. When the Coronation starts, showing all your emotions like that will get you killed."

A blush crept over my cheeks, and I quickly looked away. "Thanks for the advice," I said in a cold tone.

"No problem. You're going to need it."

I was so confused as to why a guard would be kind... and also give me advice that would keep me alive longer.

As he guided me through the halls, I tried to map out exactly where I was within the castle. There was nothing that could easily pinpoint me to where we were. Every hallway looked nearly identical with black velvet runners, paintings of the dark stone castle, and closed door after closed door. Finally, after three sets of stairs and too many endless hallways, the guard opened a door and pushed me inside.

The room was large, with a giant canopy-style bed in the center of the room. Again, there was not a single window to be seen. Golden sconces lined the wall and the flames gave off an orange glow to illuminate the room, and a plush rug was centered on the dark stone floor. When I became queen, the first thing I would do is bring light into this dungeon of a castle. But the room exuded luxury that I could have never imagined between the gold accents and dark oak furniture.

The guard shut the door and locked it behind him. Finally, he released my arm. We stood there in silence for a moment, staring each other down. Stepping closer to me, he closed the gap between us. Gently, he touched my temple, and I hissed in pain. His stare intensified towards every scrape, cut and bruise. I stared up at him frozen, drawing slow and steady breaths. So close, I could take in his delicious scent once again. For just a moment, I allowed myself to imagine us closing the gap between us. But, I could not allow that dream to stay long, for I had a battle to fight. A battle that would take every drop of my concentration and energy.

His eyes darkened, like a storm rolling over the ocean. "What happened here? Who did this?" A deep growl escaped his throat.

"Like you don't know. What do you care?" I snapped, pulling away from him. "You guards are all the same! You work for a wicked queen. To make it worse, you channel the darkness yourself, I can sense it in your veins. No good can come from you!"

For a brief moment, I saw hurt flash in his eyes. The guard clenched his jaw, staying silent, as if he was carefully choosing his next words. He pointed over to the frosted-glass double doors on the left wall. "Go bathe. You are disgusting."

My eyes widened as I looked at him in shock. Deep within me, I fought to accept what was happening. His kind were my enemy, why was he doing this? Before I could respond, he spoke again.

"I will wait out here." He turned and sat in a black velvet armchair. "You are safe within this room. No one is going to bother you. Now go." He pointed to the door once again.

I looked to the doors, then back to him. "Thank you," I said in confusion before turning towards the doors.

"Don't thank me yet, little star," he teased.

Something about that made me pause to look back at him. A smirk was plastered on his face and he offered a wink. Quickly, I turned away as heat flooded my cheeks.

Entering the bathroom, I quickly locked myself in. I pressed my back against the doors and released the breath I was holding. The bathroom was just as luxurious as the bedroom. There was a large clawfoot tub and a separate shower. Rushing over to the shower, I turned the water on as hot as it would go and shed myself of the dirty clothes from the pit, tossing them onto the floor. A soft moan escaped my lips as I entered the shower and the water hit me. Dirt and blood ran down my body as I stood under the rushing water. Once the water ran clear, I finally gave myself a proper scrubbing. There were lavish exfoliants and luscious soaps that I had never even heard of. No matter how much I scrubbed, I could still feel the dirt of the pit.

My heart broke as I thought of all the ones left behind in that terrible place as I took what should have been a relaxing shower. The tears I was holding back finally began to fall. For the first time, I allowed myself to release all the emotions that I had been ignoring.

I washed myself over and over until the water ran cold. When I exited the shower, my heart dropped as I saw the tiny black silk nightgown that was hung on the back of the door. Looking down at the floor, my old clothes were gone. A chill ran down my spine. I had no idea that anyone had entered the bathroom while I was in the shower. I kicked myself for letting down my guard, because who knew what could have happened?

Quickly, I dried myself with the soft and fluffy towel and put my long blonde hair into a braid. I stared at the nightgown for a long moment. There was no way that I was going to wear this. Especially since the guard was still out there waiting for me. I opened every drawer and cabinet, hoping to find something. There was not a single thing that could be used to cover myself.

I let out a deep sigh as I accepted my fate. Once I slipped on the nightgown, I stared at myself in the mirror for a long moment. The thin straps, V-neckline, and short hem caused way too much skin to show for my liking. But what was I to do?

Finally, I returned to the bedroom and found the guard in the same chair, reading a book. Slowly, he raised his gaze to meet mine.

"Ah, I was wondering when you were going to come out. Come, sit." He set down the book on the small oak table next to his chair, and he motioned toward the chair across from him.

I crossed my arms in front of my body and headed toward the chair. Our eyes were locked every second until I sat down.

"Good girl, I knew you could listen," he teased. Again, I couldn't help but to blush from the good girl comment and I turned my head away from him. Leaning forward, he reached out, guided my chin so that I met his stare, and his eyes darkened once again. "Now tell me *exactly* what happened to your head," he demanded through clenched teeth.

"Why do you care? Don't you want me dead like everyone else in this castle?"

He leaned back and rolled his eyes. "No one should put their hands on a lady such as yourself. Look at you; you are small and weak. Sure, you are a light bringer, but you have no idea how to use your magic. If you did, you would have used it long before now. Now, I won't ask again. Tell me what I want to know."

I bit my bottom lip and looked down into my lap. He was right. I was weak. I had no idea how to use my magic. How was I going to compete in the Coronation with no magic? Hopefully, I would reunite with Lucinda soon, and she could help me.

Looking back up at the guard, I told him every detail of what happened to me in the pit. When I informed him of the guard who hit me, a scowl crossed his features.

"What did he look like?"

I told him every detail I remembered. Luckily, when we opened the pit to let in the light, I caught a good look at him, though everything was fuzzy after hitting my head.

The guard nodded and stood. "Tomorrow you will meet the others. Rest tonight. No one will come into this room other than the servant, who will bring you something to eat. This is the last moment of peace you will get before the Coronation. Use it wisely." He quickly exited before I could say another word.

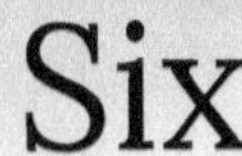 Six

S leep did not find me. Even in a comfortable bed, clean, and fed, I did not feel safe. My mind kept racing about everything that had happened and what was upcoming.

It was still mind boggling to me that I was a light bringer, and that the one person I trusted most had hidden that from me. Those ocean blue eyes haunted me every time I closed my eyes. Who was that guard, and why did he show me any kindness in a place founded on cruelty and despair. The trials ahead would be like nothing I ever faced. Every Coronation was different, so it was impossible to know what was ahead.

The guard from last night locked me in this room. After he left, I tried to sneak out to rescue Lucinda, but the door refused to budge. I felt so guilty. While she was chained to the wall in filth, I was eating a chicken pot pie, and resting in silk sheets.

Without windows, there was no telling how much time had passed, but it felt like an eternity when the door finally opened again and a new guard came in, with Lucinda.

"You two have an hour before you both will be escorted to the ballroom to meet the others," the guard said as she uncuffed Lucinda. "I will be right outside. Don't even think about doing anything stupid."

"Wouldn't dream of it," Lucinda hissed in response.

The guard rolled her eyes and exited the room, closing the door behind her.

The door wasn't even fully shut before Lucinda and I were embracing each other. She pulled away and held my face in her hands, worry filling her golden eyes.

"What happened last night after the guard took you? Are you alright?" Panic rattled her voice. "Did he—"

I cut her off before she could finish her sentence. "No, no. He brought me here, allowed me to shower, then left. He did not hurt me."

The worry on her face melted into a look of confusion. "How odd. Did he say why he would pull you from the pit early?"

I shook my head. Thinking back on it, he told me nothing about himself or his motives. I didn't even know his name.

"I am going to shower. When I come out, we need to discuss what is coming next." Lucinda turned and walked toward the bathroom.

"I need you to tell me about my magic. Why have I never sensed it?"

She stopped right before the door and looked back at me. "Shower first. I need to get the grime of that hell off of me. Then I will tell you everything you need to know."

Before I could say another word, she entered the bathroom and shut the door behind her. I let out a huff in response. Honestly, I was beginning to think that Lucinda was never going to give me the truth about my magic.

Pacing back and forth in front of the bathroom door, I tried to recall any moment in my life where I had felt magic running through my veins. There was not a single moment. This all had to be a dream, a fluke. There was no way I was a light bringer. The ceremony that declared I was, had to be wrong.

Lucinda finally emerged from the bathroom, wrapped in a towel, her blonde hair still dripping wet. She leaned against the door frame, with her head hung.

"I know you must be mad at me for never telling you the truth." She let out a deep sigh.

"I'm not mad. I'm—"

She cut me off before I could continue. "Please let me finish. I did everything for your well-being. It was your parents' last wish that I never tell you about your magic. We never expected the Coronation to happen within your lifetime. I now see that keeping you from who you truly are was wrong. It was not for your parents, myself, or anyone to decide. That should have been your choice." She raised her gaze to meet mine and stepped toward me. "Your magic was sealed away. That is why you never felt it, but I am going to unleash it now before you meet the others. I don't know what's going to happen from here on out, but you need your magic to survive. Go lay on your right side for me." She pointed to the bed.

"Is it going to be hard to control?" I asked as I made my way to the bed.

"I don't know." Turning toward the glass door, she kicked it, causing it to shatter.

"What are you doing?"

"I needed something sharp. Now lay down!" Lucinda grabbed a large piece of shattered glass off the floor.

Lying on my right side, I looked at her nervously. "Is this going to hurt?"

"It won't *not* hurt. Try to relax." She gently folded my ear and pressed the glass into the back of it.

I let out a whimper as it sliced into me. When she squeezed my ear, a scream escaped my throat. It felt as if something was tearing through my ear to escape through the cut she made.

"It's almost out," she said in a calm voice. "Take a deep breath for me. You're doing great."

"Lucinda! Please stop!" A sob escaped my throat. Before she responded, a bright flash of light flooded my vision, a wave of heat washed over me, and I heard a huge crash. The pain in my ear vanished, and I quickly sat up.

When my vision returned, I saw Lucinda on her ass against the wall. Jumping out of bed, I rushed over to her.

"Are you alright? What happened?!"

She looked at me with a grin, holding up a small piece of iron. "I got it out." She stood and hugged me. "That, Aurora, was your magic releasing itself after the last seven years of it being locked away. Do you feel any different?"

Stepping away from her, I frowned deeply. "I threw you into the wall?" Tears flooded my eyes.

"No, the pent-up magic did. I am fine, I promise." She stepped forward and took my hands in hers. "You did not hurt me. Let's get the blood washed off of you."

Lucinda wrapped her arm around me and led me into the bathroom. She sat me down on the stool next to the counter and grabbed a washcloth.

I looked down at my hands in my lap, listening to the sound of the running water from the sink as she wet the cloth. My heart pounded in my chest as I focused on the buzz that I felt under my skin.

I flinched as Lucinda gently dabbed the cloth against the back of my ear against my wound. "It's ok. It's just me." Her tone was so soft. "I remember when I turned thirteen and first felt my magic. It was like pins and needles under my skin, like a bug trying to dig its way out from under my flesh. For a while, I thought I was going crazy. But as soon as I learned how to harness and store that power, the ache for release went away." She knelt in front of me and took my hands into hers. "Close your eyes. Tell me, what do you see?"

I hesitated for a moment before I answered, not knowing what I should say. "Darkness."

"Only darkness?"

"There is a small pinpoint of light, off in the distance."

"Focus on that light, Aurora. Allow it to grow. Vanish all the darkness that surrounds you."

I did as she said, and slowly that tiny point of light began to grow. She continued her words of encouragement until all the darkness was gone and I was surrounded by golden light.

"Open your eyes, Aurora."

When I did, I looked up at Lucinda, who was now leaning against the wall across from me.

"Look at your hands." She lowered her gaze.

I did and saw a ball of golden light nestled in my cupped hands. Lucinda pushed off the wall and came over to me.

"What do you want to do with that light?"

I looked up at her and cocked my head. "What do you mean?"

"Do you want to store it away? Do you want to have it float in the air to illuminate the room? Hell, do you want to throw it at me to punish me for my lies?"

As upset with her as I had been, my stomach clenched at the thought of harming her. "I would never hurt you."

"Oh, my sweet girl." She offered me a soft smile. "Close your hands around the light. Imagine tucking it away for another time. Not dimming the light, not extinguishing it, just storing it for later."

Gently, I closed my hands, and the light vanished.

"Good, good. I knew you would be a natural. Now tell me. How do you feel?"

It was then I noticed the vibrations under my skin had stopped. While I could still sense my magic, it was no longer fighting to escape. It and I were in unison.

A loud banging on the main door caused me to jump in panic. Lucinda turned and rushed out of the bathroom.

"We are coming in!" The guard from earlier yelled from outside before opening the door. She and another woman carrying two dresses entered the room.

"These are your dresses for the feast. Get dressed quickly. We need to go, now." The guard's gaze fell to the shattered glass on the bedroom floor. "What the hell happened here?"

Seven

The music came to an abrupt stop as Lucinda and I were escorted into the ballroom. My focus immediately went up to the ceiling, which was all dark stained glass and glittered like stars. The moonlight shone through and illuminated the image of the night sky. Turning my attention back to the crowd, all eyes were on us, and it felt as if their gazes were burning through me.

The Queen tapped her glass with her sharp nail, and the ringing sound echoed throughout the room, forcing all eyes to go to her. Her dress was as dark as the void and dripped with sin. A smirk grew on her ruby-red lips.

"Don't let the light bringers ruin our fun." She walked over to a red-headed woman and pulled her close. "The party has just begun." The imposing woman slowly turned to the musicians, and after a curt nod, they continued playing.

The crowd went back to dancing, and the guard who escorted us grabbed me by my arm.

"We will have eyes on you the entire time. Do not even think of escaping," she growled.

I yanked away from her. "Wouldn't dream of it. If I ran, how would I become queen?"

Lucinda chuckled under her breath as she hooked her arm into mine. "Come along, Aurora. I see pastries, and I am starving!" She pulled me away from the guard and toward the feast.

Never in my life had I seen so much food. On top of the ten-foot-long table of pastries, there were others filled with meats, fruits, vegetables, and more. I couldn't even think about eating. The affair had me on edge, and I felt as if I was going to throw up at any moment.

Which would be a shame, because it would ruin the most beautiful gown I had ever seen. Both Lucinda and I were in white, but where she had a simple white A-line gown, mine felt designed for a princess. In the tulle of my skirt, there were thousands of crystals that glittered in the light.

I was truly a star surrounded by the darkness of this place. The floor was black marble, and the walls were matte black with embossed filigree carved into the stone. Looking around, each element was dressed in their color, and the contestants of the Coronation were in the fanciest of outfits.

As we approached the pastry table, a girl wearing a dress that looked as if it was made from water stepped in front of us, blocking our path. She offered a soft smile and extended her hand.

"When they said that there would be a light bringer in the Coronation, I didn't believe it. I'm Nova, water dancer."

I shook her hand and smiled back at her. Water magic was always one of my favorites to watch. They used fluid motions as they practiced, making each move a performance.

"Aurora. I am surprised myself, honestly."

"I heard! It's the talk of the feast. Well, that and the fact that Prince Sterling has yet to make his appearance. Have you met any of the other contestants?"

I could not figure out why she was being so friendly toward me. Soon the two of us would be enemies, and only one of us could stay alive. "I have not."

One by one, she pointed out each contestant and guardian, starting with her own guardian, Nox. He, I had heard of. Tales of his magic had spread across the kingdom. He was one of the most powerful water dancers, and I was thankful it was not him that I was up against. She then pointed to the redhead, who was currently entangled with the Queen. Zora was the guardian of the fire wielder, Elsa.

Lucinda motioned toward a woman leaning against one of the dark marble pillars, glaring at the throne. The skirt of Elsa's dress looked as if live flames danced around her. It was clear by the scowl on her face she was not happy to be in the presence of the Queen.

I was not happy to see Charoite again after our encounter in the woods. She was leaning against the far wall, watching everything like a hawk. The earth shatterer contestant, Jet, was next to her with his arms crossed. Unlike the others who were dressed to reflect their elements, the two of them were in black. His stare was locked on me. He did not even blink.

The wind weavers, Puck and Huck, were at the food tables, piling their plates high with a little bit of everything. The weavers were both very short and stout. Based on looks alone, I couldn't picture why the magic of the land would choose one of them to participate in the Coronation.

"We all met last night when we arrived at the castle. I was hoping to meet you there! Did you just arrive this morning?" Nova asked in a chipper tone.

"We did," Lucinda chimed in.

My head snapped to her, and I gave her a look of confusion.

"We had so much to prepare before coming to the castle," she continued, completely calm, as if lying was second nature to her.

"I understand! My mother hated that I was chosen. If my father wasn't my guardian, I don't think she would have let me leave." A heavy sigh escaped her. "Aurora, it's nice to meet you. I am hoping that you and I can help each other out during the Coronation," she said in a hushed tone.

"Ah, so this niceness is a ruse?" I asked. "Just to get on my good side?"

"No!" She took a step closer with fear in her eyes. "I was not made for battle. My father told me to find the strongest person in this room and make them my ally. I know the Queen is scared of you. There's a reason all the light bringers vanished. Let me help you win, in exchange for my life once you do."

My facial expression dropped as she spoke, and Lucinda's jaw fell. Clearing my throat, I raised my gaze to meet hers.

"I don't want to kill anyone. So, if you are on my team, there will be a place for you in my court."

She did not say another word. Instead, she wrapped me in a tight embrace that had me stumbling back a step.

Nox walked over and gently tapped his daughter on the shoulder. "Come along, Nova. I told you not to make this so obvious. Lucky for you, everyone's attention appears to be elsewhere." His gaze then fell to me. "Thank you, light bringer."

Nova released me and stepped back. "Sorry, you know I am a hugger! I can't help it."

Once again, the music abruptly stopped, and every light in the room went out. It was silent for only a moment before panic and screams filled the room.

"Silence! What is the meaning of this?" The Queen's voice boomed. The crowd quieted. "Fire wielders, relight the chandeliers!"

In a flash, the orange glow of firelight once again filled the space. My heart dropped into my stomach as everyone's gaze snapped toward the center of the room.

The guard from last night was no longer in his uniform. Instead, he was in an all-black suit. The only bit of color was his silver cuff links that shimmered in the glow of the firelight. He held the guard who hurt me by his hair and had him on his knees.

"Prince Sterling? What is the meaning of this?" The Queen asked, venom dripping off her tongue.

His dark ocean eyes locked onto me. "I wanted to send a message," he growled.

My head was spinning. I couldn't believe that the guard who took me from the pit and cared for me was the prince. My enemy. The one I would need to kill to rid Gaylwynn of darkness and free it from tyranny.

"This guard believed himself to be above me. I made it clear that no one was to harm the light bringer. She was my prey to hunt. But he thought it was fun to break what was not his." Sterling unsheathed his dagger and quickly sliced the guard's throat. He could not even let out a scream before the light left his eyes. Sterling threw his body to the ground and stepped toward me. "Let this be a warning to you all. Do not touch what is mine. No one will kill her but me. I will be the one to vanquish the light and return this world to beautiful shadows." He grabbed my wrist and pulled me against him. "Little star, you are mine to extinguish."

# Eight

My vision tunneled as I stared into Sterling's ocean-blue eyes. I could not believe what I had just witnessed. A high-pitched ringing filled my ears. His lips moved, but I did not hear the words that escaped them. As I tried to step back, he pulled me closer to him, and my stomach twisted into knots.

Gently, he raised his hand and cupped my face, and everything around us faded to black. The ringing that had dominated the sounds of the ball vanished, and it was now completely silent.

It was then I noticed that the darkness around us had movement. Like water, it swirled around and was tranquil to watch.

"Little star," Sterling purred. "My shadows have provided us a moment of privacy. I hope your guardian is filled with panic. These shadows are impenetrable." His hand slid down to my chin, and he forced me to look up at him.

"This is our final moment of peace. After today, when the Coronation officially starts, you will be mine."

"I will never be yours," I spat in response.

"Ah, so the kitten has teeth. Good, I like that. It would be a shame if the kill was too easy." A smirk grew on his face. "Little star, you are already mine. I have you exactly where I want you. Tonight, you are my dance partner. Tomorrow, you will be my prey."

"Y—your dance partner?" I stuttered through my words. My chest tightened, and I hated that feeling. He was the most handsome man I had ever seen, and maybe under different circumstances, I would not mind the arm around my waist and his body pressed into mine.

But this was the start of the Coronation. He was my enemy. The son of a tyrant king and a sadistic mother. For Gaylwynn to live, he had to die.

"Yes, my dance partner. For the next few moments, it would be nice to imagine what it would be like to have you in ways I can't. I am going to remove the shadows now. You will dance with me, and if you try to get free." He chuckled lightly under his breath. "My dagger will meet the tender flesh of your guardian. Do you understand?"

Breath caught in my throat, and I nodded in response.

"Good girl," he purred. The shadows vanished and revealed a silent ballroom. Everyone stood around us, just watching.

"Aurora!" Lucinda screamed.

My head snapped in her direction, and Sterling forced me to look at him. "Ah, ah, ah. Remember what I told you."

"Please," I whimpered. "Let me go to her. I will come right back for your dance. Let me tell her it's ok."

A low growl escaped his throat. "Thirty seconds." He released me and stepped back.

Quickly, I turned toward Lucinda and ran to her. Wrapping her in a tight hug, I whispered in her ear, "I'm ok. He just wants a dance. I'm going to give him what he wants to keep the peace. Tomorrow, we will go to war." Releasing her, I stepped back.

She gave me a nod and said, "I won't take my eyes off you two for a moment."

Returning to Sterling, I avoided his burning gaze. I hated how smug he looked. He won this round, but it would be the only time with me he would. Next time, I would win it all. Again, he wrapped his arm around my waist and put my hand into his.

"Did I disrupt the party?" he asked the room. "Where are my manners? Continue!"

The music resumed, and we moved with the rhythm. Neither of us said a word for the entire song. The competing emotions within me nearly tore me apart. I loathed this man and everything he stood for. Why didn't I hate his touch, his scent, or that stupid handsome face of his?

As we danced, I caught a glimpse of the queen. Anger contorted her features. Her hateful gaze was locked on us, even as Zora tried to calm her. Lucinda was standing with Nox and Nova. The three of them were quietly conversing with each other. I could not tell who looked more worried: Nova or Lucinda. Nox looked as if nothing bothered him.

"You look beautiful tonight." Sterling finally broke the silence between us.

Looking up at him, I hesitated for a moment before I said anything. "Thank you. I did not think you were the type to give compliments."

"I am when they are deserved. You have one more thing to thank me for, by the way. Better make it quick before I make you get on your knees and have everyone watch as I make you thank me properly."

"For what?" I snarled at him.

"For killing that guard. He needed to be punished for what he did to you." He snarled back.

"I won't thank you for punishing someone for hurting me when you plan on killing me yourself." I rolled my eyes.

"I will relish every moment when you beg for your life and I make you scream for me." His arm around my waist tightened, and that predatory smirk flashed across his face once again.

"I hate you," I snarled as my blood boiled.

"Not as much as I hate you, little star." Finally, he released me as the song came to an end. "As much as I loathe this ending, I must go. There is food waiting for Mother and me in our private dining room, and I am starving."

Sterling spun away and started to walk towards the exit. The next song continued, but no one danced, all eyes were still locked on us. It took me a moment to gather the words to speak after such an abrupt stop to our encounter.

"You can't eat with the rest of us? You may think you are better than everyone, but you are lower than the dirt on my shoes."

He let out a deep chuckle and stopped in his tracks. "Oh, no. You should not eat that food, either. Not all of it is edible." He pointed over to the tables.

Food was scattered on the ground. Both Huck and Puck lay dead on the floor. Blood seeped from their eyes, and foam escaped their mouths.

The Queen walked over to them, looking down at them with disgust. "Contestants. Welcome to the Coronation. Tonight was your first challenge. On the tables behind me, items were laced with poison or swapped for their toxic counterparts that could easily be spotted if you knew what to look for. Unfortunately, the air weavers did not. Know this: soon this too will be your fate. My son will be the next King of Gaylwynn and darkness will reign."

Nine

After the ball, Lucinda and I were locked in our room. As soon as the door was shut behind us, Lucinda had me tightly wrapped in a hug.

"Dear gods," she breathed. "I thought I lost you! What did that monster have to say to you when you were surrounded in darkness?"

My heart fluttered as I thought back to the interaction between the Prince and me. He was a monster. A handsome, charming monster. One that I would need to kill to win the Coronation. I could not allow darkness to win again and continue to destroy Gaylwynn.

"He wanted to get under my skin." I tried to play it off, but the truth was, he did. Everything he did tonight got the exact reaction out of me he wanted.

Lucinda gave me a knowing glare and shook her head. "For twenty years, you have had no interest in anyone. Now, a man has to kill you, and you have the hots for him. Get yourself together!"

My eyes widened in shock. I stumbled over my words for a moment before I formed a complete sentence. "I do not have the hots for him!"

She rolled her eyes in response as she sat on the edge of the bed and removed her heels. "Sure. Keep telling yourself that. You will need to for what is to come. But do not think that I did not notice how the both of you looked at each other. And I guarantee I was not the only one. Queen Serena had her eyes glued to the two of you. I am sure she didn't miss a single moment. The Coronation is going to be hard enough. Do not give yourself another battle to fight."

I avoided her gaze and sat in the black velvet armchair. Just last night, Sterling sat in this exact spot, donning the mask of someone very different from the man I saw tonight at the ball. I could not help but wonder which was the true prince or were they two sides of the same coin.

A knock startled me out of my own thoughts. Before we could respond, the door opened, and a servant entered, wheeling in a cart of food.

"Good evening. These were requested to be brought to your room, along with a note from the Queen regarding the Coronation." She bowed and quickly exited, leaving the silver cart in our room.

Lucinda got up and skipped over to the cart. She lifted the pure black envelope and removed its contents.

"Rest well. Tomorrow morning, your second challenge begins. Pray to the heavens you know how to swim," she read.

"Thank the heavens I can," I said as I made my way over to the cart. My stomach growled as I looked over the food. As I stared down at the caprese salad, I noticed another black envelope sticking out from under the plate. Lifting the plate, I grabbed the envelope and quickly removed the letter within.

Little Star,

Enjoy the food. I could not have you starving before I got a chance to watch the life drain from those golden suns you call eyes.

Your Night Sky

Lucinda snatched the letter from my hand and quickly read it over. "Oh, my heavens!" She lowered the paper to glare at me. "You need to watch yourself with the prince. I don't know what game he is playing, but you can't let him get into your head! But for now, eat. We have a long night ahead. I want you to practice your magic more before going into tomorrow's challenge."

Grabbing one of the plates, I inspected the food thoroughly. Honestly, I was not sure if I could trust it based on what happened at the ball. On top of that, if it was sent by Sterling, I definitely couldn't trust it. He made it very clear I was his number one priority in the Coronation. He would be gunning for me above all the others.

Nothing seemed out of the ordinary with the food, so I took a small bite of the ravioli, and a moan escaped my lips as the tender pasta burst open and the creamy mushroom filling coated my tongue.

Lucinda gave me a sideways glare as she took her own plate. "Calm down now," she chuckled. "At least wait to orgasm thinking of your scary murder prince until after I leave."

I nearly choked on my food. "Lucinda! That is not funny!"

She took a bite and smirked at me. "I'm not joking." She winked.

Gagging at her response, I rolled my eyes. "Okay, subject change now. Help me with my magic."

"Let me finish eating first. I am starving. I wanted to eat that turkey that was at the ball, but who knows what that was laced with." Lucinda took another bite of her food.

The two of us ate quickly, changed out of our ballgowns, and for hours into the night, we practiced calling forth and controlling my magic. By the time I passed out from exhaustion, calling forth my magic was much easier than I ever expected it to be.

Ten

Cold water being splashed on my face made me jump, and I was instantly awake. Panic filled me as I was no longer in the comfort of the palace. But instead in a small room that appeared to be underground. The walls were dark slate, and glowing blue crystals jetted out from the stone. Water slowly dripped from the ceiling, occasionally landing on my skin, causing me to shiver. There were two tunnels leading out of the space.

"Hello?" My voice echoed off the walls.

This had to be a dream, right? There was no way I was really alone in a cave. What was worse was I was still in the small nightgown that I had fallen asleep in, which provided no comfort against the cold cavern air.

From the right tunnel, Nova's voice rang through. "Aurora? Is that you?"

Bursting into a sprint, I made my way toward her. "Nova! It's me. Where are you?"

The tunnel was tight, only wide enough for one person. Some of the crystals were so long that they grazed against my skin. Lucky for me, they did not leave a mark.

"Aurora! I'm coming!" She called back.

Our footsteps and voices echoed off the cold stone until the two of us were finally in each other's view after several twists and turns of the underground path. She, too, seemed as unprepared as I was, wearing a navy silk pajama set with a tank top and pants. We wrapped ourselves in each other's arms.

"Do you have any idea what's going on?" I asked as I pulled away from our embrace.

"This must be the next challenge. I got a note last night saying that I better not be claustrophobic." She looked around the small space we were in, with a nervous expression. "And thank the heavens I am not."

"Interesting. I got a note saying that I better know how to swim." A shiver ran down my spine as another drip of water fell down my back. I hated being so exposed.

"Do you? If not, I've got you! I can control the water around you to push you where you need to go," she laughed.

"I can swim. What was back where you came from? I had another path to take back where I started that I did not explore yet."

"I awoke in the dead end of this tunnel." Nova turned to look back the way she came, and then back to me. Let's go back the other way. I'm sure that we will find out the point soon enough."

I turned and led us until we arrived at the room I awoke in. What used to be a dirt floor was now all turned to mud. My bare feet sank into its thickness.

"Grosssss!" Nova whined. "I hate mud. It's so... sticky."

I turned toward her and gave her a nervous glance. "Nova. This place was dripping water when I awoke, but the ground was dry. We need to find our way out of here, and fast."

I prayed to the heavens that I was incorrect about what I thought was happening, but I had no time to think harder about it. Grabbing Nova, I rushed into the second hallway. This one was wider than the other, and we could easily walk side by side. The ground was slick from the mud, and I nearly slipped several times as I rushed to find out where we were headed. We needed to find the exit and fast.

After about ten minutes of nothing, the tunnel finally split into six pathways, all of which were seemingly identical. How were we to figure out which path was correct? Slowly, one of the pathways illuminated with an orange glow. My heart pounded in my chest as I watched it get brighter and brighter. Nova stayed close behind me.

"Aurora," she whispered.

I held my hand up for her to be quiet and stepped forward. Heat radiated from the entrance, and my shivering skin welcomed it. Elsa, the fire wielder, finally emerged from the glow, revealing its source. Several balls of fire danced around her. While also in pajamas, at least she had shoes on. The two of us locked eyes for a long moment before she finally spoke.

"About time I finally found someone," she said in a much lighter tone than expected.

I did not get to speak to her during the ball, but I did not expect any of the contestants to be welcoming to me. Maybe she would also want to ally with me and Nova?

"Do you have any idea what's going on?" Nova's question pulled me from my head.

"I have spent the last hour searching these three paths," Elsa motioned towards the three on the left. "They are all dead ends. Zora told me about a similar challenge from the last Coronation. According to her, there are hundreds of dead ends in this place, and the first one who escaped in the last Coronation received a boon for the next challenge. And as much as I think girl power is great and all, I really need that boon, so that's all I have to say on the matter." A fireball appeared in her hand. "I am going through this tunnel." She pointed to one of the ones behind her. "And you two won't follow me. We all know you will be next to die, and I don't need you weighing me down."

My jaw dropped at her declaration. "Excuse me?" I snarled. "The two of us will be the *only* survivors. I hope you never need our help, because you've lost all the respect I had."

Nova's head snapped to me with eyes wide as I spoke.

I conjured a ball of light in my hand and aimed toward the fire wielder. "You have three seconds to get out of my sight before I end you for threatening my friend."

I injected as much venom into my voice as I could. I did not want to hurt anyone during this competition. But I would if I needed to.

"Ladies, put those claws away," that smooth and dark voice that I hated to love purred. "Elsa, did you not take what I said at the ball seriously?"

Sterling appeared out of the dark shadows of one of the tunnels. He strode over to Elsa and grabbed her wrist, which held the fire. In a blink, he twisted it, and a crack echoed off the cavern walls. Elsa screamed so loudly that it caused my ears to ring.

"I would have thought after what I did to your bitch of a cousin, you of all people would have known better."

She ripped away from him and stared up at him with hate in her eyes. "You are a bastard!"

"Ah, ah, ah. I know who my father is. Do you?" He winked and turned his gaze toward me.

My heart skipped a beat as he walked toward me. "My little star gained herself a pet. Do you really think she can help you? Nova knows nothing of hardship, of battle. I say we kill her now, end her suffering. The challenges will only get harder."

"Stay away from her," I snarled.

"Only because you asked so nicely," he teased. He stopped directly in front of me. Gently, he played with my hair as he gazed down at me with a wicked grin and a shiver ran down my back. "What a lovely little nightgown. Maybe after this challenge, I can watch you take it off for me."

My entire body tensed as he toyed with my hair. I could not stop the blush from spreading across my cheeks. All I could do was stare up at the prince.

"Get away from her!" Nova shouted from behind me, and her voice pulled me out of the trance I was in.

Before anyone could respond, the ground rumbled beneath our feet.

Sterling took a step back. "I believe that is my cue to leave. Good luck, ladies. Be mindful to stay away from Jet. He will kill you." He paused. "Well, two of you. My dog knows better than to fuck with what's mine." On that final word, he vanished into the shadows.

The ground quaked once again, this time harder. Losing my balance, I fell into the mud. No, not mud. Water. It had to be at least three inches deep. I really hoped that this cave was not filling with water when the ground turned to mud, but it seemed I had been right.

"You still gonna throw fire at us if we go with you?" I snapped at Elsa.

She stared at me for a moment. "Just stay out of my way." Turning on her heels, she rushed down one of the hallways.

Nova came to my side, placing a hand on my shoulder. "I can feel the flow of the water. It seems to be coming from here." She pointed to one of the pathways. Stepping forward, she reached down and ran her fingertips through the rising water, which now was well above her ankle. After a silent moment, she straightened her back. "Hey, Elsa!" she called out to the fire wielder. "You're going the wrong way! It's the second tunnel from the left that is the way out." She turned her attention back toward me. "We have to go, now!"

The two of us raced down the tunnel. Every time it forked, Nova led the way in what I hoped was the direction out.

The water continued to rise, and by the time Elsa caught up with us, it was at our chests.

"Took you long enough," Nova said.

"I didn't trust you. Why would you give me the right information?"

"Because Aurora and I are not your enemies. Agree to yield to our queen, and she will spare you. It's Sterling you must fear."

The fire wielder clenched her jaw and gave me a sideways glance. Before she could say another word, the water rushed us and forced us to travel farther down the path. This sudden wave caused the water to rise several inches.

"Fuck, let's get out of here. Alliances won't matter if we all drown," Elsa snapped.

With the water so high now, it was easier to swim than to walk. My arms burned as I pushed myself forward down the tunnel. After about five minutes of continuous swimming, I realized that I was not as good of a swimmer as I thought. Floating lazily down the river on a hot summer's day was a lot different from swimming for your life.

"This way! I think the exit is over here." Nova called out as we got to another fork in the cavern.

Out of nowhere, Jet came up out of the water, blocking our path. "Not so fast. Sorry, ladies."

Before any of us could respond, the cavern collapsed in on itself. Both passageways were now blocked with debris. The water now rose at a steadier pace.

Elsa pushed past us and tried to pull away the large rocks from the pile. Even with her large muscles, they barely moved.

"No, no, no!" she screamed. "This can't be how it ends!" She dove, and small bubbles gave us evidence of where she was under the water's surface. After a long moment, she sprang up and gasped for air. "They won't budge!"

Nova swam to her side. To my surprise, she looked cool as a cucumber. "Back up," she demanded.

Elsa swam over to me. Silver misted her eyes, and I couldn't tell if it was from diving below, or if they were tears of frustration.

"If we get out of this alive," she said to me quietly, "I will yield."

Before I could say anything, Nova called to us to get our attention. "Water has more power than anyone thinks." A wave then rose and crashed into the giant pile of rocks. "They think water to be soft, delicate, beautiful." The current smacked against the rocks over and over. To my surprise, the movement was localized to just around the barricade. "But water is deadly when force is applied."

After another hard push, the pile of rocks fell forward, giving us a space to cross into the passage.

"Oh my heavens, Nova! I could hug you!" Elsa squealed as she swam toward the water dancer.

"With those giant arms? You would crush my delicate bones. Save that for Jet for trapping us in here." Nova snarled and then turned her attention toward me. "Aurora, are you alright?"

"As alright as I can be," I sighed and began to swim toward her. But as I started to move, the water propelled me forward and lifted me to the opening and across.

On this side the water was much lower, only about waist deep. The top of the cavern was filled with more glowing crystals, causing this section to be much brighter.

"I got you!" Nova called out from the other side. "I know all the swimming can be rough on someone who isn't used to being in the water. As if the water was carrying her, she then appeared through the hole in the rubble.

"What about me?" Elsa called.

"You have all those big muscles! You can handle it," Nova responded.

We both watched as Elsa forced herself through the hole and over the wall of rocks. Water rose to meet her and gently carried her over to us.

"See, we are not your enemy. But making you climb over was your punishment for trying to kill us!" Nova said, splashing water at Elsa.

The fire wielder narrowed her eyes and shook her head. "The only one I'm killing is Jet. He's going to pay for trying to drown us."

"We have to get out of here to do that," I interrupted. "Come on."

Nova rushed ahead of me. "This way! We should be out soon."

She wasn't wrong. The longer we walked, the shallower the water became until the ground was dry once again. After about a fifteen-minute walk, we found the exit of the tunnel.

Cheers erupted as the sun graced our faces. Lucinda rushed over to me and wrapped me in a tight embrace. Both Nox and Zora were standing not too far behind her with smiles on their faces.

"Oh, thank the heavens," she whispered.

I hugged her back, just as tight. Looking over, Nova and Elsa also reunited with their guardians. Both Jet and Sterling were lounging in the bright green grass, soaking in the golden sun rays.

I hated that he looked so unbothered. I hated how handsome he looked as water dripped from his dark locks. I hated that his ocean-blue eyes were locked on me.

Smirking, he slowly stood and walked over to his mother. She, of course, was dressed in her signature ruby red. Sterling whispered something to her, and then her gaze snapped to me and anger washed over her face.

"It seems that everyone has made it out of the tunnels alive. Like the late King Marcellus, my son was the first to exit. He did not need assistance from others to find his way out of a seemingly impossible situation." She walked over to me and glared at me before turning away. "Two challenges down. Four more to go. Stay ready. You never know when the Coronation will turn up the heat."

Eleven

T he scent of robust coffee filled my nose and roused me from my sleep. Sitting up, I stretched my arms over my head, groaning in pain. My back and arms ached.

"Oh, good! You're awake. I was beginning to worry," Lucinda said from the bedside, drinking her coffee. She lowered her gaze to her cup. "I owe you an apology."

Reaching over, I placed my hand on top of hers and gave it a gentle squeeze. "Don't." With my body still so sore and my mind focused on what lay ahead, I had no brain power to have an emotional conversation with the only mother I ever knew.

Looking back at me, with tears now misting her golden eyes. "I should have told you the truth about what you were. Maybe I could have better prepared you."

"Lucinda! You did your best. No one expected the king to die so young. You never expected the Coronation to happen in my lifetime."

Before she could respond, there was a knock on the door. "May I come in? It's me, Elsa," she called from behind the door.

"I'm here, too!" Nova chimed.

Chuckling, Lucinda wiped her tears from her eyes and looked toward me for an answer. I nodded, causing her to get up and go open the door for the fire wielder and water dancer.

"Miss Hot Temper has something she wants to say!" Nova walked in first and immediately got into the bed with me. There was nothing I could do to stop the smile that grew on my face. I did not have many friends, but was glad to have Nova by my side.

Elsa closed the door behind her and leaned against it. Clearing her throat, she glanced toward Nova. "Don't call me that!"

"Well, cool off, and I don't need to." Nova raised her nose to the fire wielder.

For a moment, I allowed myself to think of a world where the three of us did not have to fight in the Coronation. While we definitely had trust issues, I wondered if we could have been great friends from the start under different circumstances. What else would be different if the Coronation did not exist? Would Sterling still be my enemy?

Elsa's voice pulled me from my thoughts before I let that get dangerously too far toward a certain shadow-wielding beast.

"I apologize for how I acted when I first met you in the trial. I did not realize how honorable you were. You could have left me to drown." It was then she got down on one knee and lowered her head. "Aurora Wylker, please accept my yielding. I know if you were queen, Gaylwynn would see brighter days. Sterling may think that he has won, but with the three of us, I know we can put you on the throne where you belong."

For a long moment, all I could do was stare down at the fire wielder before me. Nova was giddy with excitement, and gave me a nudge. Looking up toward Lucinda, she offered a soft smile and nod.

I did not expect so soon after the start of the coronation that I would gain two allies. Not only that, but they saw me as the best option for future Queen of Gaylwynn.

Slowly, I stood and walked over to her. Placing a gentle hand on her shoulder, I offered a warm smile.

"Elsa, you are forgiven. I am honored by your yielding and will happily accept you into my court."

It was such an odd thing to say. That I would one day have a court, that I would rule over this kingdom. Never in my wildest dreams did I expect this to happen. But it was either become Queen or die.

I was not ready to die. Nor could I allow the land to fall into darkness once again.

Excited clapping erupted from behind me. Turning my head, Nova was on her knees in bed, clapping, and smiling.

"I knew that the three of us were going to be friends!" She cheered.

"Don't get so excited," Lucinda chimed in. "The next trial will start at any moment. Who knows what will come your way."

Elsa stood. "I do. The Queen had Zora assist in setting up this challenge. I hope the two of you are quick on your feet and can handle some heat."

"Tell us everything you know," I demanded.

"Have you ever heard of the childhood game 'The Floor Is Lava'?"

Twelve

Heat licked at my skin as I looked down into the bubbling lava. Raising my gaze, I watched as the hanging platforms in front of me rocked back and forth across an open chasm. All of us stood on the edge of a cliff. The other side was nearly one hundred yards away.

Bright and early this morning, I was awakened by a trumpet and a servant entering my room uninvited. She provided me with a skin-tight pair of shorts and a just as skin-tight tank top. I felt ridiculous as I put them on. It made me feel slightly better that Elsa and Nova both wore the same thing, but the men both had on pants and a tee shirt. While their clothes weren't *as* skin-tight, they definitely showed off everything.

Terrible as it was to admit, I could not stop looking at Sterling. This was no time to crave a man, any man. Especially one who wanted me dead as we stood before a pit of lava.

"Eyes up here, Little Star. If you make it through, maybe I will show you what you need afterward." He winked.

Heat flooded my cheeks, and Elsa pulled me to the other side of her.

"Get yourself together," she said in a low growl. She raised her hand, showing off that it was still tightly wound in bandages. "He is the enemy. Once you are Queen, you can get a boy toy. Until then, focus."

The Queen cleared her throat, and we all turned our attention to her. "If the girls are done daydreaming," she snarled, "welcome to the third challenge in the Coronation. The task today seems simple: get from one side to the other. Don't get bright ideas. If you try to use any teleportation magic to move forward, you will be brought right back to the beginning by the magic of this room."

Sterling let out an audible huff and rolled his eyes in response.

"Oh my dear, Sterling. No need to worry. We all know you are superior to these rats," the queen spat. "Please turn and face the chasm. The challenge will begin shortly."

"How will we know when it starts?" Jet finally spoke up.

Elsa narrowed her gaze at him. Rage flared behind her dark eyes.

"Oh, you will know," the queen chuckled as she vanished into the shadows.

Sterling was the first to turn toward the chasm. "Well, I am not waiting to find out what that means." He walked backward several steps before running at full sprint. At the edge, he jumped into the air and landed on the first platform. My breath caught in my throat as I watched it rock and forth and the Prince steadied himself.

Jet followed behind him. As he landed on the platform, it lowered toward the lava.

The ground beneath us shook, and the edge started to crumble.

"Oh shit, we have to jump. Now!" Elsa called to us.

Nova looked at me nervously. "I'm scared. I don't know if I can jump that far."

Elsa took her hand. "You're with me. Let's go." The two of them rushed off, and the ledge crumbled beneath them as they leaped to the first platform. As soon as they landed, the platform lowered once again, bringing them closer to the lava.

Sterling was already three platforms ahead, and Jet was not too far behind him.

The ground before me continued to fall into the lava. The gap between myself and the first platform grew longer and longer. At this point, I wasn't sure if I was going to make it. I took in a deep breath of burning air and wiped the sweat from my forehead.

Gathering all the courage I could, I took a leap of faith to the first platform. Both Elsa and Nova have moved ahead, leaving me behind. Part of me was hurt by it, but I didn't blame them. We all needed to make it through the obstacles.

As soon as I landed on the first platform, a loud snap rang from above, and before I knew what was happening, one of the chains holding up the plank had fallen down into the lava. I rushed to one of the remaining chains and held on tight as the floor tilted. To my surprise, it was cool to the touch. Swallowing hard, I rocked the chain back and forth, forcing the entire platform to move. Once it swung hard enough and got me close to the second platform, I jumped to it.

Landing on my hands and knees, I let out the breath I was holding. This platform did not move at all. There was no rocking or lowering. Raising my gaze, I saw my allies ahead of me, watching me carefully.

"You alright?" Elsa called out.

"Peachy!" I laughed. "Go on, don't worry about me. Get out of here before they all start falling."

"See you on the other side!" Nova called out with a smile before the two of them turned away to continue.

I took a moment to peer ahead to see what the boys were facing. Of course, Sterling was near the end and looked as if nothing had bothered him the entire way.

Jet, however, found himself dodging large rocks that rained from above. They crashed down into the lava, causing it to rise.

I could not focus on what the others were doing. I needed to get myself through this challenge. Though I would not be the first to make it to the end, I would make it.

Standing, I quickly brushed myself off and jumped to the third area. This one was much larger than the others, by nearly double. It too did not move as I landed on it. The boards beneath my feet creaked as I walked toward the other side.

The sound of Nova's scream had my head snapping in her direction. An arrow protruded from her arm, and the stench of burnt flesh filled the air. Two more fire-laced arrows flew in their direction. Elsa, being ever so vigilant, forced Nova to duck just in time to avoid being hit again.

Very quickly, the obstacle course grew more deadly. Taking one more quick scan, Sterling was only two more platforms from the end, and Jet was mid-air, heading to his next one.

As I almost reached the end of the platform, the ground crumbled beneath my feet. Before I knew what was happening, I was falling toward the lava. In a quick moment of clarity, I grabbed onto the boards. The splintered wood dug into my hand, and I let out a much louder scream than I wanted to. Blood dripped from my palm, and I watched as it fell into the lava. Which, to my dismay, was still rising.

My muscles refused to move as I attempted to force myself up. What a time to be lacking in upper body strength. The heat made it hard to catch my breath and focus.

"What are you doing?" I heard Jet call out. "Are you out of your mind?"

The boards above me creaked, and Sterling stepped into view. He had the most smug expression I had ever seen, and it made me wish I could punch it right off of him.

Those deep blue eyes shimmered as he spoke. "Oh, Little Star." He shook his head. "I can't have you falling to your death. Where's the fun in that? Need some help?"

I snarled up at him. "I would rather die than accept your help." Still, I tried to pull myself up, but it was of no use.

A deep chuckle escaped his throat. "Well, those do seem to be your choices, but I am not done with you yet." Shadow tendrils wrapped around my body and lifted me back up to the platform. Once I was on my own two feet, they did not release me. Instead, they pulled me toward Sterling until my body was against his. My heartbeat quickened as I took in his spicy scent. Even covered in sweat, he was still too handsome for his own good. He reached down and tucked my hair behind my ear, offering me a sad smile.

"There you go, Little Star. You live to shine another day." The shadows around me vanished, and Sterling took a step away.

In a blink, he was gone. Looking around for him, he was now back at the starting area, which was now just a thin ledge.

"Well, it appears dear mother was telling the truth about teleporting. What a shame!" His voice echoed through the chasm.

Still shocked that he came back to save me, all I could do was stand there and watch him in awe as he made his way to the first and second platforms.

"Aurora!"

Hearing Nova call my name pulled me out of the trance I was in. I turned toward the sound of her voice and saw that the other three had already made it to the end.

"Come on!" she called out again.

Without any hesitation, I raced through the rest of the obstacles. Never once did I look back as I dodged flaming arrows and falling stones while jumping from plank to plank. I always expected that Sterling would pass me, but he never did.

When I crossed the finish line, both Nova and Elsa wrapped me in a tight embrace. Jet was leaning against the wall, glaring at me. His stare was so intense that if he wielded fire, I was sure I would ignite. Finally, I allowed myself to look back, and Sterling was directly behind me.

"Wonderful. We all made it." He huffed, pushing his dark hair out of his face. He looked around, confused. "I am surprised Mother is not yet here. Oh well, I suppose she will arrive soon enough. Gives us time for some fun." The look of confusion melted into that predatory grin he normally wore.

Now that I thought about it, it was off that the Queen was not here, nor anyone else. At the end of the last challenge, everyone was waiting for us at the end.

"What is wrong with you?" Jet screamed as he approached the Prince. "Why would you go back and save her?"

Sterling's face darkened. "Jet, do not make me remind you who you are speaking to," he said in a low growl.

"Someone needs to remind you who the enemy is!" Jet spat back.

"I know *exactly* who the enemy is!" The Prince's face contorted with rage, and his face grew red.

Jet staggered back in surprise, and then the prince quickly regained his composure.

Before anyone else could say anything, slow applause echoed behind us. The queen stood in the tunnel behind us, with the other guardians behind her.

"Seems you all made it once again. How unfortunate. You know, when my husband won the Coronation, two contestants died in this challenge alone. But it seems you all are refusing to kill each other for the crown. We are still awaiting supplies for the next challenge, so for the next few days, please feel free to relax and recover. Or, don't and suffer in the next challenge. The choice is yours."

Thirteen

I found myself tossing and turning, unable to get any sleep. The stress of the Coronation weighed heavy on my brain. Who knew what the queen had planned next? I wouldn't be surprised if she had us drink poison or fight a fire-breathing dragon.

Sitting up, I looked over at Lucinda, who was fast asleep. Her mouth was wide open, with a tiny snore escaping her. I did not understand how she could sleep so soundly. Though, I suppose it was not as hard for her as she kept so many secrets from me my entire life.

Getting out of bed, I changed out of my night gown into something more appropriate and snuck out of the room. Hopefully, going for a walk would help me clear some of the thoughts that plagued my mind.

The halls twisted and turned, and all of them looked the same. A noir runner with gold embroidery, paintings of places and people from across Gaylwynn, and the occasional guard wandering the halls or posted at a corner.

None of them spoke a word, but they all had their eyes glued to me.

I paid none of it any mind. The fear of what was to come weighed too heavily on my soul. The Coronation soon would come to a head, and I would be forced to make some difficult and deadly choices. While I was thankful to have both Elsa and Nova by my side, I knew when the time came, I would have to be the one to kill Sterling. Nova was not made for battle, not made to be a killer. And while I was sure Elsa would be happy to, it needed to be the light that freed the world from darkness.

If I were to be queen of this land, I would need to learn to make these hard decisions and do what was best for my kingdom. And that started with getting rid of anyone in my way of the throne.

"Isn't it a little late for you to be wandering the halls?" A deep voice pulled me from my thoughts.

I spun, and my heart sank as I realized who was only a few paces behind me. He stepped closer, and the fire of the torches reflected the anger in his eyes.

"Why did the prince save you?" Jet growled.

His question caught me off guard. To be honest, I had been asking myself that since Sterling pulled me from the prison holding area. Before I could respond, Jet took another step and repeated his question.

"He was so close to winning, but he turned around to stop you from falling. When he learned I had trapped you in the cavern, he punished me." He lifted his shirt, and half of his torso was deep purple from bruising. He threw down his shirt and took another step closer.

My heart pounded in my chest. I was frozen with fear. The rage in his voice sent a shiver down my spine. Every time I tried to answer, my mouth would open, but no words would come out.

"Do you know when the Coronation started, he told me I was on my own? For the last thirty years, I have stood by his side. Always his loyal dog, doing whatever he asked! What is it about you that makes you so special?" He reached out, grabbed me by my throat, and slammed me into the wall. "Say goodbye, *Little Star*," he mocked. "Once you are gone, there will be nothing in my prince's way to claim what is his destiny."

His hands tightened around my throat, and I tried to gasp for air. Tears welled in my eyes as my body refused to react. As he tightened his grip, making it impossible for me to breathe, spots filled my vision. I could not allow myself to go out like this. What was wrong with me? Why could I not move? I searched deep within for my magic, praying it would come to my rescue.

As everything grew hazy, a bright flash of white filled my vision, and Jet released me and let out a scream. Falling to my knees, I gasped for air. The earth shatterer finally took a step back from me, writhing in pain. Looking up, half of Jet's face was bright red and bubbling. Staggering and still gasping for air, I forced myself to my feet. He stared at me with deep hatred as I stepped toward him.

"I don't know why he saved me. Just know I would never offer him the same courtesy," I spat. "Here is a little piece of advice. Join me or join his fate. This is your only warning."

Before he could respond, I walked away from him.

Fourteen

The dining hall was full of nobles from across the kingdom. They were all here to watch the Coronation unfold. Sterling and Jet were missing from the room, thank the heavens. After last night, I didn't know if I could face Jet again. The chill in the air had no one questioning the scarf I wore that hid the red marks around my neck.

Elsa, Nova, and I sat together with our guardians in a far corner of the room. However, that did not stop anyone from watching our every movement.

"Have you guys heard when the next challenge will be?" Nova finally broke our silence as she stuck a piece of fruit in her mouth.

"Soon," Zora responded coldly.

I did not know much about Zora. Other than she was the leader of fire wielders and Elsa's aunt. She did not speak much around us. According to Elsa, she did not speak much at all, unless there was something important to say.

"I heard from the queen they are waiting for one final shipment that's coming from overseas before the next challenge can begin," Nox added. "Though, no one I have spoken to seems to have any clue what it is."

Using my fork, I pushed the food on my plate around. It was hard to have an appetite not knowing if this would be my last meal.

"Hopefully we have a few more days," Lucinda finally spoke. "We need more time to work on Aurora's magic," she whispered.

Zora glared over at her. "You did that one a disservice."

Lucinda's head snapped toward the fire wielder. "I did what I thought was best. Don't forget it was *you* we came to for help when her mother fell pregnant. But you did not want to get involved!"

The room fell silent. All eyes were on the guardians as they bickered about the past. Zora's face fell, and she avoided Lucinda's gaze. "I had a family of my own to protect. It was a hard time for all of us."

"How about we talk about this somewhere more private?" Nox cut in. "Somewhere the *entire kingdom* isn't watching." He looked over at Elsa and me, who sat watching with our mouths wide open. "Girls, I am sorry. Please enjoy your lunch."

With that he stood, beckoning the other guardians to do the same and leave with him. Everyone watched as the three of them exited the room. It wasn't until they were long gone that the hall filled with voices once again.

Elsa turned toward me. "Aurora," she whispered. "I am so sorry."

"Don't be. I have come to terms with what Lucinda did. Gaylwynn is not a safe place for my kind. But after I win, it will be. No longer will anyone have to make those hard choices, for Gaylwynn will be safe for all who reside within its borders."

Shadows accumulated at the end of the table, and a deep chuckle escaped them. Sterling emerged from the shadows, that predatory grin on his face.

"What a lovely little speech. Too bad it is nothing more than a fantasy. Though maybe if you yield, I will keep you as my pet. I would love to force you to watch the land return to darkness."

I straightened my back, refusing to look away. "You are confused, *Sterling*." Never again would I refer to him by his title. He held no power over me, and I needed him to know it. His lip twitched at the sound of his name, and a smile grew on my face. "Soon, the kingdom will return to normal. Sunny days are to come. Make sure to put on sun protectant. We wouldn't want that fair skin of yours to burn."

He let out another chuckle. "No, I suppose not. That must have been what happened to Jet, no? Too much time in the sun yesterday? I will be sure to tell him next time to bring extra protection," he sneered back.

My heart dropped, and my eyes widened. Unable to control my face, he won this round of the game we continued to play.

Finally, he removed his gaze from me, and it landed across the table at my friends. "You two may want to be careful. Wouldn't want you two to fly too close to the sun as well, lose your wings, and fall. There is always time to return to the sweet caress of the night." Quickly, he snapped his attention back to me. "Who knew such a little star could burn so brightly?" On that final word, he turned and walked away.

Refusing to look away, I watched until he exited the room. I squeezed my hands together tightly to stop them from quivering. In an instant, the girls were up from their side of the table and sitting by my side.

"What was that about?" Nova whispered in my ear.

Elsa quickly jumped back up, pulling me with her. "Come on. Let's get out of here." She turned her head to the crowd, who watched us closely. "This is your future queen, not a jester for your entertainment! Mind your manners, because I never forget a face," she sneered as she pulled me close and rushed us out of the room. Nova followed closely behind us.

Whenever we tried to speak, Elsa would cut us off, telling us that it was not yet safe. Finally, she pulled us into her room and shut the door behind us.

"What did you do to Jet?" Elsa asked immediately after closing the door.

"Why would you assume she did something? You know Sterling is crazy!" Nova responded.

Sitting at the edge of the bed, I looked up at them, with tears in my eyes, and told them the entire story as I removed my scarf. My two friends watched in horror as I told them how Jet had tried to strangle me.

"I'll kill him." Elsa's tone sent a shiver down my spine. "I will set him ablaze and end his miserable life."

"If the prince doesn't kill him first. We all saw what he did to the guard for touching her," Nova added and then looked at me. "Did you know Sterling before all this?"

"Nope. The first time I met him was when he pretended to be a guard and took me out of the pit."

Their faces dropped. "You were in the pit?" They asked in unison.

I had totally forgotten that at the ball, we had told every-one a different story about our arrival. But, now that we grew close, I knew I could trust them both with the truth.

I nodded. "I didn't know he was the prince until he showed up at the ball and made his grand declaration."

"What happened after he got you out of the pit? Did you sleep together?" Nova asked.

Heat rose to my cheeks. "Dear gods, no! We just talked. That was it."

"Do you know why he is so obsessed with you?" Elsa came and sat by my side.

I shook my head in response. "I wish I knew. This game we are playing is driving me insane."

Nova came and sat on the other side of me. "Do you want to sleep with him?"

"Nova!" Both Elsa and I shouted.

"What? Don't act like the tension isn't there," she laughed. "He's hot. You're hot. If you weren't in a com-petition that demanded that you kill each other, it would have totally happened already."

Rolling my eyes, I laid back on the bed. "You're insane. You know that?"

"But that's one reason you love me." She laid down on her side next to me.

Turning my head, I smiled at her. In such a short frame of time, I considered these two my best friends, and I was so lucky to have them by my side. In my village, Lucinda and I kept to ourselves. To be honest, I don't think I ever had friends like Elsa and Nova. And now that I had them, I had to make this world better for them.

Together, we would make Gaylwynn a better place.

The three of us stayed in Elsa's room until the moon was high in the sky. I was so envious that her room had a window to the outside. Once we all were yawning, we finally decided to say our goodbyes. Before I exited Elsa's room, I made sure to put the scarf back around my neck to hide the markings.

Nova's room was in the other direction from mine, so I walked the castle halls alone. This time I made sure to be on full alert.

After about ten minutes of walking the halls, I realized I had no idea where I was. Everything looked so similar that it was hard to tell exactly where I was. After a few more moments of wandering, I heard some familiar voices from behind a nearly shut door.

"What is wrong with you?" the queen spat. "Have you lost your mind?"

"No. I am fully sane." Sterling chuckled.

His laugh was cut off by a hard slap. Slowly, I inched my way to the door so that I could listen closely.

"The longer you let her live, the more of a mockery you make of your father's legacy. He did not want the light bringers around for a reason. Instead, you kill your own men and save her from death? Why? Why do you betray us this way? This is not what you were meant for."

There was a long moment of silence before another word was said.

"Mother," he growled. "The next time you lay your hand on me will be your last. Once I am king—"

"If you become king. At this rate, you would allow that bitch to take the throne. We have worked too hard to allow you to screw it up. Lucky for you, you have a mother in a high place who loves you. I have secured her demise in the next challenge."

The hair on the back of my neck rose as a chill ran down my spine. A million thoughts raced through as I imagined what horrors the Queen would throw my way.

"What do you mean?" Panic rose in his voice. "She is mine to kill!"

"You are taking too long. So, I have ensured she will no longer be an issue. Remember this. For if you dare to defy me again, it will be your last mistake. Even when you are on the throne, remember it is me who put you there, and that my allies lurk in the shadows."

The sound of heels clicking against stone had me rushing away from the door and ducking behind a statue. The queen stormed out of the room and thankfully in the opposite direction from where I was hiding. Once she turned the corner, I quietly walked into the room.

It was an expansive library. It had six tiers, and the ceiling was made of frosted glass. The railings on each tier were matte black and gold. There were too many bookshelves to count. All of which were fully stocked.

On the first floor, there were several tables. Some were clear, and some were stacked with books. But the one that caught my eye was the one Sterling was sitting on.

His hard stare was locked on me and said nothing as I slowly approached him. I wasn't sure why, but I sat down on the table next to him. We sat in silence for some time before he gently put his hand on top of mine and gave it a gentle squeeze.

Why was I not disgusted by his touch? Why was I not pulling my hand away? Why was he being so quiet and calm compared to his normal obnoxious self?

His shadows slithered across the floor and shut the door. Once they were, he finally broke the silence.

"How much did you hear?"

"I didn't mean to eavesdrop! I—"

"How much did you hear?" He cut me off, asking again with a snarl.

Looking up at him, I brought my hand to his slightly red cheek. "Does she hit you often? Why would you allow her to do that?"

He grabbed my hand and pulled it away from his face. "It's complicated. When I killed my father, I couldn't bring myself to kill her too. She at least pretends to care. Marcellus clearly only ever cared for himself and the power he gained."

Jumping up from my seat, I stared at him in awe. "You... *You* killed the king?"

That familiar smirk returned to his face. "You seem surprised. You have seen what I'm capable of. You are not the only one who wishes for a better future for Gaylwynn."

I scoffed. "Really? Coming from the man who declared he would be the only one to kill me. You want better for the kingdom?"

He pushed off the desk and closed the gap between us. With his arm around my waist, he pulled me close. He used his free hand to lift my chin until our gazes locked.

"Do not think you know my intentions based on my public actions. I know the role I must play until the time is right. Just know, Little Star, I want better for this world."

He leaned down and gently brushed his lips against mine. Gods, I hated how soft his lips felt against mine. What I hated even more was the fact that I kissed him back. My heart pounded in my chest as he lifted me, spun around, and sat me on the table.

My legs wrapped around his waist as our kiss deepened. My fingers ran through his dark locks and I wished I could freeze this moment. Fireworks went off inside my chest, and for the first time everything felt too right.

Too good.

Too soon, he pulled his lips away from mine. His ocean-blue eyes shimmered as he looked down at me. For the first time, he offered me a genuine smile.

"Why must my enemy taste so sweet?" he purred.

Heat rose to my cheeks, and I stared up at him speechless. When he reached for my scarf, panic filled me. Quickly, I grabbed his hand and forced it away.

He chuckled nervously. "I can see how hot you are. Your face is bright red. Take the scarf off."

"No!" I blurted out.

He tilted his eyes, and amusement changed to concern. "No? Why?"

In a scramble to come up with an excuse, one of his shadows grabbed the scarf and ripped it from me.

Anger contorted his face. "Who did this?"

"It's nothing. I handled it!" I pushed him away and stepped toward the door.

Sterling grabbed my wrist and pulled me back to him.

"You handled it?" His eyes widened. "When Jet told me you randomly attacked him, I knew that didn't make sense. Tell me exactly what happened. Tell me now!"

Yanking away from him, I shouted back, "Why do you care? It doesn't matter."

"It matters more than you know. Tell me," his tone softened. "Please?"

We stood there for a moment in silence, staring into each other's eyes. Tears welled, as I could not believe the version of the Prince of Darkness standing in front of me. I did not even think the word 'please' was in his vocabulary. Nor could I understand why he cared so much for me.

A nobody from a small village. A light bringer cursed to be his eternal enemy.

He was everything I wasn't, but in this moment it felt as if we were made to be one.

Finally, I told him everything. His jaw clenched tight as he held himself back from interrupting me. When I was done, he let out a deep breath, stepped forward, and wrapped me in a tight hug.

"He will never hurt you again. I will make sure of that."

Looking up at him, I caught him wiping his eyes. "Why do you care so much about this?"

He released me, stepping back. "Do you need me to walk you back to your room? It's late. I am sure Lucinda is worried about you."

Why wasn't he answering my question? "No. I can find it myself from here."

"Very well. Good night, Aurora." He walked past me, exiting the library, never once looking back and still clutching my scarf in his fist.

Fifteen

Ten potion bottles of various colors and sizes were in a neat line on the table in front of us. There was something about the only white bottle that drew my attention. I found myself constantly looking at it. Our guardians sat on the far side of the room, watching silently, except for the queen, who stood just on the other side of the table.

"Before you, there are five potions with positive effects and five with negative effects. Choose wisely, because this could greatly affect you in your next challenge." From thin air, a red velvet bag appeared in her hand. "In this bag, there is a stone for each of you. It will reveal the number that you will select your potions in." Slowly, she walked over to Nova and extended the bag to her. Nova reached in and pulled out her stone. Peering over, hers had the number two. The queen disregarded me and moved on to Elsa, Jet, and Sterling. Only after they had chosen, she returned to me, with a serpentine grin. She extended the bag to me without a word. Reaching in, I pulled out the last stone. Rolling it over in my hand, I revealed the golden five painted on it.

"Well, there you have it. Jet, Nova, Elsa, the Prince, and then Aurora. Once you select your potion, hold on to it. You will drink them together." The queen joined the other guardians across the room.

Jet stepped forward. After a few minutes of smelling and staring at each potion at least three times each, he selected a square amber bottle. Nova then examined all of them, and quickly she decided on a light blue tube. Elsa took the longest of them to decide. She spent nearly five minutes with each of the remaining bottles before selecting a red, circular one.

All the guardians watched in silence. The queen never once pulled her gaze away from me until her son stepped forward to select his potion.

Before he could even finish his first step, he tripped and fell onto the table, knocking over a potion in a white star-shaped bottle that I had been fixated on. It crashed onto the floor, and a foul scent spread across the room.

The Queen's face contorted in anger as she jumped from her seat. "No!"

Sterling stood and brushed himself off. "These damn stones. They must be uneven. What a shame. Mother, is everything ok?"

She sat back in her seat, trying to relax her face. She clenched her fists so tight that the whites of her knuckles showed. "Just fine," she said through her teeth. "Hurry up and make your selection."

Sterling walked to the black square bottle and immediately selected it. He turned back toward us and offered me a wink before getting back in line.

"Aurora," the queen snapped. "Make your selection."

I stared at the bottle on the floor. The pull I had was no longer there. I could not help but think of the conversation I overheard between the queen and Sterling. Was whatever she had in that bottle meant for me? Was that the demise she planned?

Quickly, I gave the remaining four bottles a glance and chose a green bottle before returning to the line.

The queen stood and stepped forward. "Wonderful," she sneered. "Now that you have made your selection, on the count of three, you will all drink at the exact same time. I wish you all the best of luck."

One.

Two.

Three.

We all swung back our potions at the same time. As soon as the liquid hit my tongue, my entire body filled with a tingling sensation. Darkness surrounded me, and to my surprise, I did not panic.

Why did part of me wish that it was Sterling taking us away from this damned place? Why did I crave a refuge like he provided at the ball?

When the darkness faded, I found myself in a dark and dense forest, alone. The only light was the gentle white glow emitting from my skin.

Sixteen

"**H**ello?" I called out.

The only response was the distant song of a bird and the leaves rustling in the wind. Wandering through the woods, I continued to call out for anyone. Leaves crunched against my boots as I stepped over large roots and fallen logs. I prayed to the gods that I would find Nova or Elsa. I was terrified of what would happen if I saw Jet or Sterling first.

The branches twisted around one another, making the canopy so dense that no sunlight could get through. I used my own glow to navigate around the roots that bulged from the ground. The bird song vanished, and the forest grew eerily silent.

The hair on the nape of my neck stood as a chill ran down my spine. The loud crunching of leaves and thundering boom of entire trees hitting the forest floor made me spin around. I stared in horror. Entire trees were swallowed by total darkness.

Staggering back and tripping over one of the twisted roots, I stared up in horror as bright red eyes appeared within the void.

A roar so loud that my ears throbbed shook the trees, and rows of sharp teeth appeared in the void. The darkness condensed into a monstrous form and jolted toward me. Its clawed feet tore through the roots below, sending dirt flying as it ran.

My entire body screamed as I forced myself off the ground. Without hesitation, I ran in the opposite direction of the beast. My eyes darted from the ground to avoid the fallen logs and roots, to the path ahead of me to avoid running into trees, and back at the monster that pursued me. It used its massive clawed hands to rip entire trees out of its way.

The tears in my eyes nearly flooded my vision, making it harder and harder to see. With quivering hands, I brushed them away. This was like nothing I had ever faced, and I prayed that I could be back in my small village basking in the sun.

I could hear its vicious snarls growing louder as it gained on me. It sounded as if it was directly behind me. Looking back, I was thankful that it was not as close as I thought it would be. It was then, my foot caught on a mound that was hidden under leaves. Slamming into the ground, I let out a wail.

It was then I realized what, no *who* I had tripped over. Jet lay on the forest floor, fast asleep. Drool escaped his lips and onto the ground beneath him. Shaking him, I tried to get him to wake. Looking at him, at the monster that was still approaching, and back at him, I screamed for Jet to move.

I hated Jet, but I could not abandon him to the beast. No matter how much easier my life would be once he was gone. Trying to pull him to his feet was an impossible task. There was no way I could lift his muscular frame.

I had only one choice.

Standing, I moved forward. Calling all my magic within me, the faint glow around my body brightened intensely. The darkness around me was gone and had been replaced with blinding white light.

An ear-piercing screech echoed off the trees. When the light dimmed, the monster was gone. In a panic, I looked around, praying to the gods that it was gone for good. When the birdsong finally returned to the forest, I released a sigh.

Turning back to Jet, I looked down at him, shaking my head. A gentle snore escaped him as I leaned down and gave him another good shake. Again, he did not respond.

It was then I realized that whatever potion he drank must have knocked him out cold. He was lucky I found him before the beast did.

"Aurora?! Was that bright light you?"

Nova's voice had me jumping up, looking around for her. She was not anywhere in sight.

"Nova?" I called out. "Where are you?"

"I'm right here!" She sounded as if she was right next to me.

"Right, where?" I continued to search around for her, peering behind a large tree.

"Stop pretending you can't see me!"

Something wrapped around my wrist and tugged gently. Yanking my arm back, I stared at the empty space in shock. Slowly, I reached out, and my hand met a solid mass.

"Uh, we are close," she nervously chuckled, "But not grab-my-boob close."

Again, I yanked my hand away. "Oh, sorry! Nova, you are completely invisible."

"No, I am not! Stop playing!" She huffed back at me.

"I swear." The space in front of me was completely vacant.

"Oh, my gods," she squealed. "What do you mean?"

"Calm down. You don't want to draw any attention to us. These woods have monsters. Nasty ones. I'm lucky I am still alive. It must be from the potion you chose."

The sound of gentle crunching leaves led away from me and over toward Jet.

"What's his deal? This doesn't seem like the greatest place for a nap."

"I assume his potion put him to sleep. I need you to help me get him out of the middle of the forest."

"You want to help Jet? He left us to drown, remember?"

I let out a sigh. "I know, but I refuse to be like them. When I am queen, I will rule with kindness and mercy. That needs to be at the forefront of everything I do."

"You are going to be the best queen Gaylwynn has ever seen."

Even though I could not see her, I could hear the smile in her voice.

"There is a cave not too far from here. We could put him in there for now. Just until we find Elsa and our potions wear off."

I couldn't help but worry about my second friend. She was the strongest of all of us and could handle anything that came her way. For now, I needed to focus on getting Jet out of danger. Grabbing him under his arms, I lifted his chest off the ground.

"Get his feet and lead the way."

Jet's legs rose into the air as Nova let out a groan. "This...way..." she strained.

Luckily, it was a short walk to the cave. Any longer, and I wasn't sure that I was going to be able to carry him. Gently, I placed him down, but his feet fell hard.

"Nova!" I scolded.

"He doesn't deserve your kindness, Aurora." There was a silent moment before she continued. "I wonder what happened to his face. I'm sure the prince had something to do with it. What a sick bastard."

Looking up at the cavern ceiling, I hesitated before I responded. "It was me. He attacked me in the hall after we left Elsa's room the other night."

"Oh, my gods. He attacked you, and you're still helping him? You are a much better woman than I am." She let out a deep sigh. "And *that* is exactly why you need to be queen."

Walking over to the cave's entrance, I looked out into the forest. Wondering exactly what the point of this challenge was. Was it to find the exit, or is there a hidden temple deep within where a riddle needs to be solved?

Turning back to where I thought Nova was, I asked her to tell me everything she saw in the forest before we met up. According to her, nothing unusual stuck out to her. It was just dark forest and this small cave.

Exploring was the only way we would truly find out what was happening in these woods. The two of us walked for what seemed like over an hour, seeing nothing but tree after tree.

We stayed as silent as we could, trying not to gain the attention of any more monsters within the forest. We used whistles that mimicked the bird song to communicate. Since I couldn't see Nova, every few moments she let out a soft tune to help me figure out where she was.

The forest seemed endless. Everything looked the same, and I was beginning to lose all hope of ever finding Elsa or escaping the forest. Nova let out a little whistle, and I turned in the direction of the sound.

"What do you think we should do?" I asked with a huff. "This isn't working. I swear I have seen this tree at least three times."

Before Nova could respond, like a prayer answered by the gods themselves, Elsa appeared directly in front of me. She looked around frantically, and her eyes went wide when she saw me.

"Aren't you a sight for sore eyes!" She wrapped me in a hug. "I hate this place! I can't stop teleporting. I'm so glad you're safe, but if I vanish, know that it wasn't on purpose."

"Elsa!" Nova squealed.

The fire wielder looked around, with the same look of confusion I had when Nova and I first met up.

"Invisible," I sighed. "I'm beginning to think none of those potions had positive effects."

Elsa laughed. "Well, it just saved my ass from some beast."

"You have seen the monster?" My eyes went wide.

She gave a small nod. "Hopefully I never do again. I was lucky that I teleported away just before it got to me."

"I'm thankful not to have seen it yet," Nova added.

"You should be!" Elsa said, looking around again for the water dancer. "I'm going to have nightmares about it for weeks."

"Elsa, do you have any idea why we were brought here? All we have seen in this damned place is the monster and tree after tree." I sat down on a large log, finally relaxing now that the three of us were together.

She shook her head. "No. Honestly, that is all I have seen as well. No sign of Jet or Sterling. I'm sure they got some sort of unfair advantage over us."

Nova let out a chuckle. "Our future queen found Jet. And in pure Aurora fashion, saved him from the monster."

Elsa shot me a surprised look. "You did? Why would you do that?"

Shaking my head, I sighed. "Because... I don't know. I felt bad. Just because I hate him and he's a jerk, doesn't mean he deserves to die."

"Aurora." Elsa's tone grew cold as she looked at me with a down-turned expression. "He wouldn't have done the same for you. He wants you to die. Not everyone deserves kindness. Many will take that kindness and use it against you. Where is he now? You saved him, and I'm sure he ran off without a thank you!"

"The potion he drank put him in a deep sleep. He's tucked away in a cave somewhere nearby."

Looking around, I tried to remember which way led to the cave. But everything looked the same, and at some point, I had gotten turned around. As I was searching for the way I came, and the three of us finally stopped talking, it was then I realized that the birds had gone quiet. My stomach dropped, and a chill ran down my spine.

"We have to go! Now!" I jumped up from the log. "It's coming!"

Before we could even take a step, the forest darkened around us. A deep growl shook the trees, and from the void, those red eyes appeared once again, locking onto Elsa and me. Again, the widespread darkness formed into a two-legged beast. It did not hesitate and sprinted toward us.

Elsa grabbed me tight by the arm, pulling me with her as she ran into the forest. Right as we started running, she vanished into thin air. Both Nova and I called for her at the same time. The only reply was the monster's snarl.

I pushed my body as hard as I could, trying to get as far as I could. This time, I made sure not to trip over any roots. I knew my magic would free me from this chase, but it refused to answer my call.

Looking back, the monster split into two. One of them continued after me, and the other went in another direction. I called out for Nova, but she did not respond. Panic riddled my bones, and I prayed that her invisibility kept her safe.

Finally, I felt the warmth and tingle of magic under my skin under my command. Not allowing myself to stop running, bright white flashed. The monster's scream rang out behind me. When the light faded, I looked back to see if I was still being chased. All I saw was the endless sea of dark trees.

Once I was sure the monster was gone, I finally stopped running. Hands on my knees, I tried to catch my breath. Endurance was never my strong suit. Once I could breathe easier, I called out for Nova.

There was no answer.

Even as I went in the direction where I saw the second beast, there was no sign of Nova. The birdsong returned to the forest, and I started to use our whistle signal in hopes she would respond.

Still, there was nothing.

For what seemed like hours, I wandered deeper and deeper into the forest searching for my friends. Too easily I got turned around in these woods. Everything looked the same, and there were no landmarks to help me determine where I was.

Luckily, there were also no further signs of the monsters that stalked these woods. My magic was still not responding to me the way I needed it to. I could not help but wonder if that was due to the potion that made me glow, or if I still needed more time to attune myself to my abilities.

"I never thought you would take your nickname so literally," Sterling's deep voice pulled me from my own thoughts, causing me to jump. He grabbed my wrist and spun me to face him.

Looking up at him with wide eyes, I was stunned. Until he spoke, I had no idea he was so close.

He let out a chuckle. "Little Star, you should pay close attention. There are worse monsters than me in these woods. Ones that would be all too happy to feast on your gorgeous flesh."

Leaning down, he slowly dragged his tongue up my neck. My body quivered in response, and I bit down on my bottom lip to hold in my whimper.

"Sterling, what are you doing?" I was finally able to force words out.

"For the first time, I have you all alone. I don't need to worry about who is watching or listening. Go ahead and take a guess at what I have planned for you." His head rose from my neck, and he looked down at me with a predatory smirk.

As I tried to pull away, he held me tighter. I pressed my hands against his chest, pushing as hard as I could, but it did not matter. Sterling was stronger than me, and there was no way I could force myself out of his grip.

"Let me go! This is not the time for this," I pleaded.

"This is the only time we may have before our little game is over. You were made to be mine. Just as I was made to be yours." He slammed me into a tree and pressed his body into mine.

The air electrified around us as I looked into his blue eyes. I hated how much I loved them. How I wished I could dive in and escape the world we found ourselves in. I hated that we were enemies and that to free Gaylwynn he would need to meet his end.

Most of all, I hated how badly I wished he would kiss me again. Biting my bottom lip, I couldn't help but crave his touch.

As if he could read my thoughts, he pressed his lips against mine, and I saw stars. Forcing his tongue into my mouth, our passion intensified. His spicy scent took over me, and my legs grew weak. When he finally released my wrists, I wrapped my arms and one of my legs around him to pull him in closer. Yes, I'd just been trying to push him away, but this man drove me crazy in every way. I both loved and hated how I wanted him as close to me as possible. One of his hands found its way to my ass, and he grabbed it firmly. There was no part of me that wanted him to stop.

Too soon, he pulled away, looking down at me with a longing expression.

"Why do you have to be my enemy?" I whimpered.

"Because the dark must consume the light. That's how it has always been. Though, I can think of another way I'd much rather devour you." He leaned down and kissed my neck once again. This time, I did not stop the moan from escaping my lips.

"If I had the time," he said in between kisses. "I would start with this neck." His free hand found its way to my breast and gently grabbed it, pulling another needy whimper from me. "Then I'd kiss and lick all the way down your beautiful body." His hand continued to travel down until it met the fabric of my pants.

"Sterling," I breathed.

"Shh, Little Star. Let me have my moment." His hand slipped into my pants and found its way to the apex of my thighs. "You are so wet for someone who is supposed to hate me," he teased. His fingers gently slid across my slick entrance, and I panted while squirming in his grasp.

Heat flooded my face as he found my bundle of nerves and rubbed against it. Pleasure coursed through me as he applied more pressure.

No, I was wrong before. What I hated most was how much I loved his hands on my body and how I craved more.

"Sterling, what—"

Before I could finish, he cut me off with a searing kiss that stole my breath. As the passion intensified, he slipped two fingers inside me. Pleasure I never knew before today continued to build within me as he slowly pumped in and out and his thumb massaged my clit. As I reached for his pants, he grabbed my wrist.

"Not yet, Little Star. As eager as you may be, I owe you much more pleasure for what you have been put through. Only once my debt is paid, will I allow myself an ounce of satisfaction."

"You are nothing like what I thought you would be," I moaned.

"And you still have much to learn."

As his thumb flicked against my sweet spot, the pleasure that had been building finally erupted. Stars filled my vision as euphoria washed over me, and the glow that surrounded me intensified.

Sterling leaned in and gently kissed the top of my forehead. "Such a good girl."

I looked up at him, completely hopeless. Even after our talk in the library, I was still trying to convince myself that I could defeat him to save Gaylwynn. But now I knew the truth.

There would be no way that I could ever harm him. As much as I hated to admit it, I allowed his shadows to wrap around my heart and root himself.

"Get off of her!" Elsa's battle cry echoed off the trees.

In an instant, she pulled him away from me. His face shifted to a sinister expression. He brought the two fingers that had forever changed my world to his lips and slowly dragged his tongue over them, releasing a deep groan.

"What a shame. I was hoping to play with you a little more before our fun was ruined," he purred.

"You are disgusting!" Elsa rushed over to me and wrapped me in a tight embrace. "Are you ok? I am so sorry I wasn't here sooner to stop him!" She spun away from me, and fire formed in her hands. "For too long you have lived a life where you think you can just take and take. It's time someone put you in your place."

Sterling let out a chuckle. "Oh? Is that so? Elsa, you need to mind your own business."

She threw fire at him, and he stepped out of the way just in time. The tree behind ignited. He turned his head to the raging flames, and his laugh intensified.

"Oh, well, that will certainly piss off the beast. Good job. At least there are two of you who can fight it off once it arrives. Hopefully, the little water princess shows up soon before we all burn to a crisp."

The second fire in her hand vanished, and she looked at Sterling, horrified. "What? Don't want to stay when the times get tough? This is why you can't be king. You are a coward!"

Sterling's smile fell, and his cold stare fell on Elsa. "You think so little of me for someone who knows nothing.

Maybe you should ask your friend the truth about me before you continue to judge." Elsa's gaze widened, but before she could say anything, he continued. "The potion I drank silenced my magic. Yeah, I throw a mean punch, but that doesn't do too well when fighting shadows."

Stepping to Elsa's side, I quickly spoke. "What do you mean that the fire will piss it off?"

This was not the time to have the conversation that he was trying to instigate. But I would need to tell Elsa and Nova the truth that he was not our enemy.

Sterling turned toward me but refused to look me in the eye. "This forest is under its protection. He knows we are threats, and that's why the beast hunts us. He won't stop until we are all dead, or it is."

That's when the forest grew silent. Even the roar of the flames was muffled as darkness surrounded us. In an instant, Sterling was at my side. He leaned in close and whispered so quietly that I could barely hear.

"If you want to run, I will distract it. I don't want you to get hurt."

Looking up at him, sadness and concern welled in his ocean eyes. Turning toward Elsa, all her focus was on the darkness as it formed into the beast and the flames returned to her hands.

"I would never abandon my friends," I said firmly, stepping forward.

Elsa looked toward me and smiled. "Hope you're ready."

This time, my magic was eager for my call. It tingled under my skin, begging for release. The monster's ruby eyes focused on Elsa as it split in two.

Throwing her flames, the beasts easily dodged them. Heat washed over my body as more of the forest caught fire. Focusing all my magic, a beam of light escaped my palm and shot forward. It hit one of them in the arm, and it wailed in pain, but it did not stop the beast from rushing closer.

Just as one of them pounced on Elsa, she vanished. While I was thankful she was safe, I hated now that I was alone fighting these two beasts.

The fire continued to spread to the trees around us, and smoke filled my lungs, causing me to cough hard. Trying to call for the explosion of light, my magic did not respond. I knew that if I could expand my glow, we would be safe.

I expected Sterling to be gone when I looked behind me, but he was grabbing a large stick and sticking it into the flame that now surrounded us. He waved it in the air like an extra-long torch, calling for the beasts. Sweat beaded on his temples, and the fire's glow illuminated the fear on his face.

True fear. My heart nearly shattered as I saw it in his eyes. For the first time, the prince, who was so sure of everything, who could defeat anything, was afraid.

And if he was afraid, what did that mean for me?

Both of the monsters stopped and turned their attention toward Sterling. In an instant, they were rushing toward him.

"Was that smart? You said you don't have access to your magic!"

He looked toward me and gave me a smile that did not meet his eyes. "Run, Little Star. Be free before shadow and flame devour you."

My heart skipped a beat in my chest, and magic roared under my skin. I would not let Sterling sacrifice himself for me. As one of the beasts slashed him with its long claws, leaving black wounds, my magic finally erupted.

It was all directed directly at the beast that tore at my once enemy, the man I was supposed to hate. But, no. I didn't hate him at all. For when he was in danger, true danger, rage fueled me. As my light hit the beast, it screamed as it vanished into thin air.

Once it was gone, I rushed toward Sterling, who now lay on the ground, black blood spilling onto the forest floor. I couldn't help but focus on his chest, which too slowly rose and fell.

A loud growl from behind me made me jump from my skin. In my panic, I had forgotten about the second monster. Spinning toward it, my eyes went wide. It was so close that I could feel its hot breath. Horror rang through me as it raised its clawed hand. Just as it swiped down, Elsa appeared between the monster and me. She turned toward me, for just a brief moment with fear in her eyes. She turned back to the beast with fire in her hands, ready to strike. But, the beast was too fast.

Her scream would haunt me until the day I died. By the time her body hit the ground, the only sound was the beast's growls as it continued to attack her.

All I could do was stand there in horror as the world slowed around me. Blood flew into the air off of the monster's claws. Tears poured down my face as a sob finally escaped me.

The flames around us withered until we were surrounded by scorched earth. My body refused to move as I watched the beast bite into Elsa's arm. She didn't move. She didn't make a sound.

Why wasn't she fighting back? I didn't want to think too hard about it.

If I stayed frozen, I would meet her fate.

That familiar tingle of magic returned and intensified more than I could ever imagine. The glow around me grew brighter. That light grew, twisted and transformed until it almost mirrored the beast.

My creature wasted no time. Once it was fully materialized, it rushed the shadow. In a clash of light and dark, the two beasts were a mangle of tooth and claw. But the shadow was no match for my creation.

For, in the end, light will always overcome the darkness.

The fangs and claws retracted from the creature of light. For a long moment, it stared down at the once-strong fire wielder, then over to the Prince.

When it finally looked back at me, my heart broke from the sorrow in its eyes. Before I could do anything, it burst into thousands of tiny white orbs. They floated in the air and illuminated the forest. The clouds finally parted, and the sun warmed my face. Looking up, the dense canopy was now burned away and ash gently flew through the air.

The trees that survived the fire were now bright green, and the birds continued their song. Flowers bloomed on the vines that wrapped around the trees, and the forest floor was full of lush foliage.

Rushing toward Elsa, I fell to my knees and wrapped her in my arms. I couldn't look into her eyes, for I feared what I wouldn't see in them. A sob escaped and shook me as I held my friend close. We may not have known each other very long, but I couldn't imagine a world without her. Thinking about that future caused so much pain as if my heart was being torn in two.

The Queen's scream rang through the forest. Turning my head toward the sound, I saw a scene that mirrored my situation.

For the first time, the queen was on her knees and sobbing.

"Someone help him! He is all I have left in this cursed world!"

One of the guards at her side immediately knelt and lifted Sterling off the ground and blood dripped onto the ground. He said something to the queen that I could not hear over the sobs that echoed off the trees.

In an instant, Sterling and the guard vanished into darkness.

The queen's attention then turned to me. Her face twisted in anger as she forced herself off the ground.

"You have been lucky so far, light bringer. But your luck is coming to an end. For the final challenge will be your last," she sneered. Turning to her guard, she continued. "Find the others. Their potions should be wearing off now. Return them to the castle if they are still alive." She then looked back at me. "If they have met their end. Leave them here to rot."

Darkness filled my vision, and when the light returned, I was in the throne room, covered in blood. The queen sat on her throne, looking down at me with a twisted smirk.

Elsa was gone.

Seventeen

Nova and I both lay in Elsa's bed. Any moment, the guards were going to kick us out and empty this room. But for one final time, we wanted to lay in this bed and pretend she was still with us. That Elsa would come through the door and give me a hard time for my longing glances toward the prince, or tease Nova for being the girliest of us all. Her amber and honey perfume still clung to the sheets.

Nova looked up at me with tear-filled eyes. "I can't believe she's gone." She stood and walked over to the dresser, opening the top drawer.

"I know." I was haunted by the image of her final moment, and the sound of her screams replayed in my head over and over. Walking over to Nova, I leaned my head against her shoulder. Nova twiddled a golden ring with a ruby between her fingers.

"Girls," Zora's firm voice called from behind us.

We both spun toward the fire wielder guardian. Her face was stoic, but there was pain seeded in her eyes. We all stared at each other for a long moment, not saying a word.

"I wanted to thank you both," Zora finally spoke again.

"Thank us?" Nova and I said in unison.

The fire wielder nodded. "In all our years, never did I see Elsa step out from the wall she surrounded her heart with. For the first time, she made true friends. She saw a better future ahead if you were to win the Coronation." She joined us at the dresser. "Please take something to remember her by. Allow her fire to always burn in your heart."

We stayed in Elsa's room until the guards came. Nova said she needed time alone, so she returned to her room. I found myself wandering the halls, deep in thought. It had been three days since we had returned from the forest, and part of me wanted to check on Sterling.

I would be lying to myself if I wasn't worried about him. The image of him near death on the forest floor flashed in my mind, and pain rang through my chest. I could not believe that the man who declared to the kingdom that he would kill me sacrificed himself so that I could live. Between him admitting to what he did to his father, the conversation between the Queen and him that I overheard, the spilling of the potion, and most of all the passion that grew between us in those woods, had my thoughts spinning.

"What are you doing in this part of the castle? It is off-limits to visitors!" A guard's voice pulled me from my thoughts.

Looking around, I realized I had wandered into a section I did not recognize. I stared up at the guard with wide eyes. "I am so sorry," I said in a sweet voice. "I just got turned around."

He narrowed his eyes. "Do not lie, light bringer. I am sure you have come to slay the prince while he is unwell."

"I would never stoop so low!" My heart ached at the thought of causing Sterling any harm after everything that had happened between us.

Stepping forward, he grabbed me by my arm. "No need to test it. Let's go." He pulled me with him as he started walking down the hall. Panic welled in me, I couldn't understand why this guard would help me.

He held on firmly but did not cause any pain. After a few moments of walking in silence, I finally asked the question that had been at the forefront of my mind.

"Is he going to be okay?"

He looked down at me with disgust. "I am sure you would be displeased by the news that he is expected to make a full recovery."

A sigh of relief escaped my lips. This man would never know how thankful I was to hear those words. I could not stop the smile that grew on my face.

The guard cocked his head and stared down at me with a sideways glance. "You look happy for someone who is going to be killed by the prince once he recovers. Have you finally submitted to the dark, or have you lost your mind?"

I did not respond to him. In all honesty, if the smile made its way back to the queen, I worried what she would do. I was still so confused by her. She seemed to want her son on the throne, but when I heard them in the library, it sounded more like she wanted a puppet. Her reaction in the forest was not what I expected. Never did I picture Serena as a caring mother.

The guard escorted me back to my room. When we were in front of my door, he finally released my arm.

"If I catch you in a restricted part again, I will not be as kind. Be thankful it was me who found you. Other guards may not have been so gentle." He turned and began to walk down the hall.

"I'm not afraid of the guards. Did you forget what happened at the ball?"

The guard stopped and turned his head toward me. We stood there for a moment in silence before he spoke. "Not all of us are loyal to the prince, or the throne. You may want to keep that in mind." He turned away and continued down the hall.

"What do you mean?" I called out to him.

Never once did he look back.

The tingle of magic danced under my skin. It ebbed and flowed as I tried to control it. After the forest, I knew that my number one priority before the next challenge was trying to get a full grasp of my powers. I could not risk being in a situation where it did not respond to my call. Still being new to my magic, I did not have it under full control.

I couldn't help but imagine what would have happened if I had been just a little faster. If my magic killed both beasts before it was too late. Before I lost my friend.

Before I almost lost the man I...

No.

Pushing those thoughts down, I returned my concentration to my magic. I had to stay focused. Love had no place in my heart until I was on the throne.

But if I was on the throne, Sterling would be dead.

"Aurora, your glow is fading," Lucinda said.

Opening my eyes, I looked up to meet her gaze. She stood at the bedside, watching carefully.

"Sorry," I sighed. "I got distracted."

She shook her head and sat by my side. "Want to talk about it?" Lucinda placed her hand on my knee.

I shook my head. "Not really."

"Is it about what happened in the forest? You could not have predicted that Elsa would teleport there at that moment. There is nothing you could have done."

Wiping the tears from my eyes, I nodded. "But if I had killed the monsters before that—" Lucinda cut me off before I could continue.

"No. None of that. The what-ifs will eat you alive." She looked away from me and gave a deep sigh. "Aurora, I need to ask you something, and I need you to be honest with me."

Panic filled my chest as my heart beat faster. "What is it? I will always be honest with you."

"We were all watching. We had a crystal ball that would show us what was happening in the woods. It was focused on you when Sterling first found you. It moved onto Nova once Sterling licked your neck, and when it returned to your point of view he was being attacked by the shadow monsters. What happened in between that time, and why did you not seem upset that the Prince of Darkness, *your enemy*, was touching you?"

My heart pounded harder in my chest with every word. I stared at her for a long moment, not sure how to respond. Lucinda would never understand my feelings for him, but I could not lie to her. Taking a deep breath, I finally admitted the truth, not only to her but to myself.

"I love him."

Her jaw fell. In a split second, that look of shock twisted into anger. "Aurora! He is playing you for a fool. Do not forget what happened at the ball. He will kill you just to take the throne."

"You're wrong. There is so much that you don't know, that *I* don't know! He wants what's best for the kingdom.

He's saved me twice now, once during the obstacle course and once in the forest."

Standing, she shook her head. "You're letting him make you weak. Remember why we are here. Remember what the dark lurkers have done." Lucinda walked over to the bedroom door. "I can't even be in the same room as you right now!"

"He isn't like them!" I stood, stepping toward her. Tears in my eyes, I could not believe she would not hear me out about this. Why didn't she trust me? She should know that I would never put her or this kingdom in danger.

Placing her hand on the door handle, she looked back at me. "You need to get out of whatever spell he has you under before it is too late and you end up like the rest of our family."

She turned back to the door, exited, and slammed it behind her.

Eighteen

It had been two days since our fight, and I had not seen Lucinda. I was not sure where she was. Even Nova and Nox had not seen her, at least that's what they told me.

Tossing and turning in bed, sleep did not find me. Throwing off my blanket, I stared at the ceiling for a long moment. Again, my thoughts were flooded with worries for Sterling. He still had not made an appearance since the forest, and we had been back for about a week now.

Getting out of bed, I quickly got dressed in the darkest clothes I could find. I needed to see him, and I would not take no for an answer. Leaving my room, I silently crept down the hall and made my way to his wing. Carefully, I dodged every guard by hiding in nooks and corners.

Finally, I arrived at a set of double doors that were as black as the void with swirls and filigree engraved on them. One door was slightly open, and I peeked inside.

My eyes immediately focused on a large four-poster bed with sheer black drapery. A dark figure sat in the center of the bed. Shadows leaked from the bed, forming into tendrils. They opened the curtain, revealing Sterling, shirtless.

"Well, well," he said gently, "I didn't expect you to come calling. Come in before someone sees you."

Looking around to make sure the coast was clear, I stepped into his room, and once inside, the door shut behind me.

My eyes locked onto his, and my heart melted. He was bruised, but he was alive.

"I wanted to make sure you were okay." I looked down at my feet to escape his predatory stare.

"It's cute how much you care." He stood from the bed, and the blanket that was covering his bottom half fell onto the dark flooring.

I could not help but raise my gaze slightly as I discovered that he was in nothing more than his boxers. Heat flooded my cheeks as the Prince slowly walked toward me.

"Well, now that I see you are well, I should go." I took a step back.

"Why?" He stopped directly in front of me and grabbed my chin, forcing me to look at him.

"You know why," I said softly, but not weakly.

"Then you shouldn't have come. Because I won't let you leave until we finish what we started."

His lips gently brushed against mine, and a shiver ran down my spine. In reflex, I kissed him back without a second thought. Our kiss intensified until we were a clash of tongues and teeth. He held me so close to him that I felt his considerable length harden against me.

Against my deep desire, I pulled away. "Sterling," I whimpered.

"Little Star," he tsked. "Don't you dare allow yourself to think that I will allow you to stop now. You deserve all the pleasure and more that I will provide you. I am not sure how much longer I will survive without making you mine."

I tried to pull away, but he lifted me and held me against him before spinning around and tossing me onto his bed. Sitting up on my elbows, I whimpered once again as he stared down at me with a predatory grin.

"I cannot allow you to have me," I declared. Even though there was nothing more I desired than to surrender myself tonight and allow him to devour me.

He crawled into the bed until his face was inches from mine, his expression growing more ravenous. The air was electrified around us as heat ran through my body. "I wasn't asking," he whispered just before slamming his lips onto mine and forcing me to fall back onto the bed.

His hands found mine and pinned me to the mattress as we kissed. It was too easy to submit to his kiss, to slide my tongue into his mouth. Too easy to give in to the growing tension between us.

His hands slid down my body to the hem of my shirt. He toyed with it for a moment before he ripped it from me, tearing the fabric, and threw it onto the ground. I did not stop him. I had spent too much time restraining myself from the man I craved most. As he pulled down my pants, he smirked at me as he slid down my body.

"Good girl," he purred. His hand found its way in between my thighs and gently rubbed against my aching slit. "You are already so wet for me."

I stared down at him, my lips refusing to move. I knew that this was wrong; Lucinda was right. Only one of us would make it out of the Coronation, but I could not stop him. Would not stop him.

I needed the Prince of Darkness more than I needed air.

When he pulled my legs apart and feasted on my core, a moan finally escaped me. The ecstasy had me fully relaxed for the first time in a long time. How I wished we could stay like this for eternity. Gripping the sheets, I wrapped my legs around his head, pulling him in close. As he sucked on my clit, I squirmed from the overwhelming pleasure.

His mouth pulled away from me, and he slowly licked my essence off his lips. "You taste divine, Little Star, as if you were made from sunshine and honey."

"Is that so?" I teased.

Sterling slowly slid two fingers inside me. When he removed them, they glistened with my juices.

"You tell me."

He brought them to my lips and pushed them into my mouth. From the moment he and I met, he promised I would be his. For too long I fought it, and I thought that I would hate this moment. But, everything felt so right. How could submitting to him be wrong? Looking up at him, I gently sucked on his two fingers, cleaning my sweetness off him. He was correct, sunshine and honey.

Pulling his fingers from my lips, he plunged them back inside my aching pussy. This time pumping them in and out.

"Sterling!" I cried.

"Tell me how you taste," he demanded.

"So sweet," I moaned louder as he toyed with me. His thumb pressed against my clit and rubbed in tight circles. Squirming under him, my body could not handle the edge of desire and ecstasy I was being pushed to. Shadows wrapped around my wrists and waist, pinning me to the bed, and forcing me to accept the pleasure the prince offered.

Just before I reached my climax, he removed his fingers from me, and rose to his knees. A deep need seeded inside me, as his warmth left my core. I craved more of him.

"Oh, Aurora," he purred. "I have thought about this moment ever since I first laid my eyes on you." He slowly removed his boxers, revealing his considerable length.

My eyes went wide. It was much larger than anything I had ever seen, and my mouth watered at the sight of it. An ache in my core grew as I craved to feel it inside me.

"Sterling," I breathed, looking up at him.

He leaned down and gently brushed his lips to mine. "If you really don't want me to, I will delay this a little while longer. Just know, I *will* have you."

"No, I want this more than I should. It's just—"

He cut me off with another kiss. "Nothing else matters right now. It is you and me. Focus on that." His tip prodded my entrance and gently ran up and down my slit. "Focus on us. How right this feels. Anything that goes on outside those doors doesn't matter now."

Pushing in his tip, I stretched around him. Too slowly, he worked himself in and out, pushing in a little more each time until he was fully inside me. Arching my back, delicate moans escaped my lips. My whole life I was taught to fear this man, but how could I fear someone that made me feel this good.

Once he was halfway in, he picked up pace. As he thrust deeper inside me, the pleasure built up within. For the first time, I experienced a true euphoria like nothing I had ever known. Once he hit my innermost wall, my eyes rolled back.

Abruptly, he pulled out just before I exploded in bliss. "Not yet, Little Star, not until I am done with you."

The shadows lifted me into the air and flipped me. Landing on my hands and knees in the bed, I gazed back at Sterling. He reached forward, grabbed my hair, and yanked it, forcing me to look forward.

"I hope you are ready. That was just a warm-up." He drove back into me harder than before, causing me to scream in delight.

Quivering around him, my body fully submitted. I needed everything that I could get from him. Every drop of pleasure, as if it was a drug. The tighter he pulled my hair, the closer I got to that edge of satisfaction I was so desperate to cross. Pushing back against him, I wanted to feel him as deep inside me as I could.

Sterling gripped my hip with his other hand and thrusted so hard that I fell forward onto my stomach. That did not stop him from continuing to claim me. He leaned forward, pressing his front to my back. The hand that held my hair slid around my neck and squeezed.

My eyes rolled back as euphoria washed over me more intensely than I had ever experienced. My entire body quivered under him.

"Who do you belong to?" He moaned in my ear.

"You," I admitted. As much as I hated it, it was true.

"Good girl." He pushed in as deep as he could and released into me.

It was so hot and deep inside me, warming my core.

When he pulled away, warmth leaked from my core. Sterling grabbed my hips, forcing me back to my knees. He ran two fingers up my slit, collecting what was leaking, and pushed it back into me.

"Don't you dare waste a single drop," he growled.

The sounds of the rain hitting the window and the roaring fireplace nearly had me to sleep. My head rested on Sterling's chest, and he gently petted my hair. We had been like this for hours after our... *rendezvous.*

I was torn between my heart and my duty. I loved him. I loved a man who shouted to the kingdom that he would be my end. But underneath it all, there was a soul who wanted what was best for his kingdom. We were on the same team. Rising onto my elbows, I looked down at him and took a deep breath. He sat up and cocked his head.

"What is it?" He finally broke our silence.

"We need to talk about what this means. What happens now?" My chest tightened as anxiety filled me.

Sterling stood from the bed, his back facing me. "My mother is going to announce the next challenge in two days. You could yield. I can promise you and Lucinda a good life, away from here. You two can live safely and comfortably in the countryside."

My heart sank. "You want me to yield so you can send me away?" My voice cracked as I spoke, and tears welled in my eyes.

"I don't see any other options," he said coldly.

Getting out of bed, I found my clothes and put them on. My shirt was torn down the center, so I tied it together so that I was somewhat covered. "And what if I refuse to yield?"

Sterling did not answer, and my already hurting heart shattered into a million pieces. Without a word, I spun and ran out of his room. I ran until I was back in my own.

Lucinda sat on the bed, awaiting my arrival. She jumped up and looked at me with a concerned expression. "What's wrong?"

Quickly, I wiped away the tears and gritted my teeth together. "Nothing," I snarled. "Can we keep going over my magic? I need to be ready for whatever is next."

Nineteen

Three days passed since I had seen Sterling. Most of the time I had spent with Lucinda working to control my magic. It was the best thing for me now to concentrate on, instead of my broken heart. Even when I wanted to push past my limits, Lucinda forced me to take breaks. She said with the next trial looming, I needed to be ready for anything.

When the announcement from the Queen about the final trial didn't come yesterday, I added that to the pile of lies he told me. But the tightness in my chest would not vanish, as if I was on the edge, waiting for our fates to be told.

I never told Lucinda why I came crashing into our room with tears in my eyes. Thankfully, she didn't pry. Nor did she bring up our fight about Sterling. I could not handle telling her she was right about everything. Part of me thought she knew, but was too kind to rub it in.

My stomach growled as I walked into the dining hall. The aroma of roasted lamb caused me to salivate. My heart sank when I did not see Nova in the crowd. Instead, it was just the pompous nobles who all looked down at me.

Did they ever stop to think about what would happen once I am queen? Once we are no longer in a game for their entertainment, how quickly will they turn from mocking gawkers to bowing at my feet begging for anything I will give to them?

I was so thankful that we had a section solely for members of the Coronation. I was not sure I could handle mingling with the nobles. It was hard enough having them watch my every move.

Sitting down at an empty table, I placed my elbows on the dark wood and held my face in my hands. The chatter of the nobles turned to a buzz in my ears. My chest tightened as I tried to push out all the noise.

"We must stop meeting like this," Jet's voice pulled me from my own thoughts.

Lowering my hands, I made sure he could see me roll my eyes. He stood across the table, looking down at me in a way he never had before, soft and concerned. Half his face was still scarred from my magic, but it had healed much more since I last saw him in the forest.

"May I sit?" From behind his back, he pulled out two glasses and a bottle of wine. "I've come with a peace offering."

I furrowed my brow and motioned for him to sit. He did not hesitate to take the seat directly across from me and pour two glasses. Sliding one over to me, we sat there in silence for a long moment.

Clearing his throat, he finally spoke. "You could have killed me in the forest, but you didn't."

I nodded, staring at him intensely. Swirling the glass of wine, he looked down at the liquid. When he looked back at me, he shook his head.

"Why? Why would you do that? After everything I have said and done. You had your chance to remove me from the Coronation, but instead, you gave mercy."

Finally, I picked up my glass and took a long sip. The bold, bone-dry taste washed over my tongue. It was no surprise that this would be what Jet chose. It matched his personality.

"When I am queen, this will be a kingdom of mercy, a kingdom of second chances," I said, taking another sip.

"Don't be a fool. Gaylwynn is set in its ways. After centuries of being ruled by the dark, there is no kindness left in this place!"

Setting my glass down, I offered a soft smile, shaking my head. "See, Jet, that is where you are wrong. For in the darkest times, kindness grows. Even when others try to snuff it out, there will always be a friend who will have your back. Or a stranger to offer a hand in their time of need. A rival that offers mercy when it's undeserved. It takes one seed of kindness for it to grow and bloom. When light reigns, kindness will too."

His eyes widened as he leaned back in his seat. "You really are something else, Aurora. I see why the prince is so in love with you."

Scoffing, I took another sip of the wine. "He doesn't love. He is the Prince of Darkness. He only cares for one thing: the crown."

The room darkened and fell silent as the queen walked in with the prince and Nova behind her. Confusion washed over me, I could not imagine why the two of them would be with her. As soon as she was through the doors, the water wielder rushed over to me.

"Why are you coming in with them? I hope they aren't giving you any trouble." As I went to take another sip of my wine, she smacked the glass out of my hand. It shattered on the floor.

"Tell me you didn't drink any of that yet." Concern filled her eyes.

Jet stood, walking over to Nova. He offered her a wink, then turned his gaze to me. "That too-trusting attitude of yours will be your undoing. Good luck in the final challenge." He strode away, joining the queen and prince, who stood in the center of the room.

"No, no, no!" Nova sobbed.

"What is it?" My stomach turned as the fear in her eyes grew.

"Silence!" the queen commanded, her voice booming off the stone walls.

Everyone's attention turned toward her, and the hushed whispers through the crowd fell silent. A wicked smirk grew on her face as she locked her eyes on mine.

"The time has come. Too long have we allowed the Coronation to be silly games. It is time for the king to take his throne. Come all to the arena and watch the Prince of Darkness claim what is his."

Pure darkness filled the room. Nova clung to my arm, but the void was so dense that I could not see her. Just as quickly as the darkness came, it was gone.

Nova and I now stood in a large arena with Jet and Sterling on the other side. The walls of the ring were so tall and slick, there would be no crawling out to escape. Above us were row upon row of filled stadium seats. The nobles in the dining hall, who were watching our every move, now had a front-row seat for whatever happened next.

The queen sat on a throne-like seat in a private box away from the nobles with her two guards standing at her side. Seated with her were Lucinda, Nox, and Charoite. Both Nox and Lucinda looked more nervous than I had ever seen them. The earth shatterer looked smug, as if she knew some deep secret.

Nova sobbed into my arm. I looked down at her, wrapping an arm around her.

"It's going to be ok. We are going to get through this together. I know it's hard without Elsa, but we've got this!" I tried to encourage her. I made a promise that I would protect her, and I planned to keep it.

She looked up at me, her eyes red and swollen. "The wine was poisoned. It had the same concoction in it that Sterling drank during the last trial. They tried to make me give it to you, but I refused! You won't have your magic for days."

My heart sank as I looked over at Jet. A low growl escaped my lips as he stared at me with a smirk. I wanted so badly to wipe it off his face.

"Citizens of Gaylwynn," the queen said, her voice echoing through the arena. "You have all waited for this moment. Trust your next king will do what is right." She stood, walking to the edge of her platform. "Competitors, this is your last chance to yield to your future king. Where do the loyalties of light and water lie?"

"My loyalties lie with the people of Gaylwynn. I will do what I must to free them from you," I said loudly.

"So be it." She turned back to her throne. "May the last one standing be crowned king."

Twenty

The crowd fell into an uproar. All I could do was stand there, frozen. I was in total shock that the final trial was now, and that I was so careless. While not having any magic was not ideal, I would do what I needed to protect Nova, to save this kingdom. My chest tightened as I tried to steady my breath.

The ground rumbled beneath us, and my gaze shot to Jet. He had lifted a large chunk of the ground into the air with his magic, and my eyes went wide as it barreled toward us. Grabbing Nova, I ran across the arena, my feet sinking into the sand, causing me to move slower than normal.

The mass of rock landed next to us, barely missing Nova as it crumbled, returning to pure sand. Nova let out a loud sob, looking up to me with panic in her eyes. I grabbed her by the shoulders and forced her to look me in the eye.

"I need you to get it together! You are the only one with magic between the two of us. You need to do exactly as I say if you want to make it out of here alive."

Neither of us was prepared for a battle to the death. And poor Nova was not made for war. But for now, we both needed to become whatever we needed to survive.

She looked as if I had given her a firm slap and gave me a quick nod. "I'm sorry. You're right. We can get through anything together." Her face hardened with determination.

Looking over at the men, I was shocked to see them yelling at each other with anger seeded in their tones, but I could not make out the words they were saying.

"They are distracted. Hit them hard. Hit them fast. Keep out of reach," I said firmly.

"Understood, but first..." She raised her hand into the air. The ground beneath our feet grew damp and hardened. "There we go. Now it should be a bit easier for us to move around."

With a wave of her hand, a ball of water formed from thin air, split into three separate globes, and darted toward the men.

Right before it hit them, they stopped arguing and dodged out of the way. Sterling's eyes finally met mine, and they were filled with sadness. Which was quite different from the rage that was plastered on Jet's face.

"You have been nothing but a problem from the moment you were brought to the castle," Jet called out to me.

He slowly approached, and with each step he took, the ground rumbled. "I don't know what type of spell you put the prince under, but it ends now!"

Jagged pieces of earth rose and shot at us as if they were sharp daggers. Nova and I weaved in between them, but the wet sand caused me to slip. One of the pieces sliced into my arm, and I let out a cry.

Nova spun toward me, crying my name and reaching out for me. But before the third syllable left her lips, one of those sharp stones slammed into the side of her neck. Her face immediately fell blank as blood leaked from her lips.

A scream escaped me as I scrambled toward her. I held her close, sobbing, and begging for her to stay with me. Weakly, she raised her hand and brushed her fingers against my cheek.

"Long live the Queen of Light. I wish I could have lived to see the better world you promised," she whimpered. On that last word, her hand fell limp. Nova's eyes glazed over, and I watched the last bit of light leave them.

A roar shook the arena. Looking toward the sound, guards were dragging Nox away, kicking and screaming. The throne was on its side, and the Queen stood with her hands over her mouth as two guards consoled her.

"Send him to the pit!" She demanded. "How dare he attack me!"

I could not worry about what was happening above the arena; I was still in the fight for my life.

Gently, I laid Nova on the soft ground. Using two fingers, I closed her eyes for her. Looking to the sky, I sent a prayer to the gods as tears rolled down my face. I promised her that we would survive this mess and I would give her a kingdom she could be proud of.

I may have failed in protecting her, but I would never fail again. I would make sure that the better world I promised would come.

Standing, I faced Jet. The smug little smirk on his face intensified the anger that welled up inside me. Taking a single step forward, he finally spoke.

"What will you do now, Aurora? You have no magic. You have no friends to save you."

"I will kill you," I snarled.

Holding his stomach, he burst into laughter. "With what?" Bending over, he grabbed a handful of sand. When he straightened his back, he allowed some of it to run through his fingers. "Sand? You must have forgotten only one of us can use the earth as a weapon." The ground rumbled once again. Directly in front of him, the ground cracked. The fissure shot toward me and expanded. "When I'm done with you, they will inscribe on your grave 'Here lies the last light. A fool who tried to outshine the dark'!"

Out of nowhere, Sterling appeared behind Jet, his eyes black as the void and shadows flaring around him. Jet froze, looking forward in terror. The growing fracture in the ground stopped several feet before me.

"You have disrespected our queen for the last time." Sterling's voice was so cold it sent a shiver down my spine. But, his words rang in my mind over and over.

Our queen.

With a blade forged of shadows, he sliced Jet's neck. Blood sprayed across the arena. Staggering back, I stared in horror at the violence before me.

The crowd grew louder, cheering on the Prince of Darkness. They demanded that I be his final victim. Sterling pushed Jet's dead body onto the ground, and our eyes locked.

Those black eyes shifted to the blue I hated to love. My chest tightened, and the world slowed around me. Step by step, the prince grew closer. The dagger in his hand vanished, and sadness grew in his eyes. All I could do was watch him as the crowd called for my blood to be spilled on the sand.

When he opened his mouth, I expected him to ask me to yield, but I could not have predicted what was to come.

"I, Sterling Vespero, Prince of Darkness, yield."

The crowd fell silent as Sterling took a knee and bowed his head. Staggering back, I stared down in shock at the prince. Words tried to escape my lips, but they came out a quiet jumbled mess.

He looked up at me through his brows. "Long live the Queen of Light!" he declared, loud enough for the arena to hear. If it weren't for the burning pain in my sliced arm, I would think this was a dream.

In front of me, in a burst of bright light, appeared a crown that looked as if it was crafted from golden rays of sunlight. It hovered before me, and deep within I felt a pull towards it. Even as my soul called to the crown, I looked back at Sterling, who was still kneeling.

"What are you doing?" I quietly asked him, hoping that no one else could hear me.

The Queen appeared in a shroud of shadows next to Sterling, pulling him to his feet. "Yes, what *are* you do-ing?" She seethed. "I silenced her magic for you. You were handed the crown, and you threw it away?" She turned her burning gaze toward me. "For *this*?"

"For your Queen," Sterling corrected.

She snapped her attention back to me. "She is no queen! I am queen! Guards seize her!" Serena grabbed the crown but quickly recoiled from it with a cry of pain. Her hand was now seared, matching the burns I had given Jet that night in the hallway.

Stepping toward the crown, I stared at it. That pull toward it grew stronger as it sang my name. Once I touched the crown, bright light filled the arena once again. When I placed it on my head, a warm glow washed over me. Looking up toward the crowd, all eyes were on me. Every single person in the stands bowed. Tears welled in my eyes as I took in everything that had happened. I did what I promised, and made sure the dark no longer terrorized Gaylwynn.

Not a single guard stepped forward, and Serena looked around in a panic.

"What are you doing? You cannot allow the light to win! Seize her at once!" she demanded again.

Again, not a single guard moved. Turning my attention toward Serena, it was I who now grew a wicked smirk.

"Your time has come to an end. When this all began, I told you that light would overcome the darkness. I promised a better world to the ones I care most about." I motioned to the crowd. "A better world for all of you, the people of Gaylwynn. No longer will night reign in terror. Guards!"

"Yes, my Queen?" They answered in unison.

"Seize them. Serena and Sterling both. Silence their magic and send them to the pit. Show them the darkness that they have forced upon others and let them rot in it."

To be continued...

Also by Willow Asteria

The Blood Singer Trilogy
https://amzn.to/3KO4erc

The Realms of Elswyth
https://amzn.to/3xsvM2r

Learn More Here!